A Joy-Filled Christmas

Rachel Anne Jones

A JOY-FILLED CHRISTMAS

ISBN: 978-1-955784-19-1

Published by Satin Romance
An Imprint of Melange Books, LLC
White Bear Lake, MN 55110
www.satinromance.com

Published in the United States of America.

Cover Design by Ashley Redbird Designs

I dedicate this book to first and foremost, my wonderful husband Douglas and my three amazing children, who always believe in me, as well as the Kapfer-12, mom and dad Jones, Sandy, Chris, Sabina, Kris, Amy, Candy, and Stacy.

I also dedicate this story to my parents and Aunt Mary, who never knew a stranger and welcomed more than a few in over the years.

I dedicate this story to all my female family members who enjoy a good love story—sorry men. I dedicate this story to the entire Quest family who have shown me there's always room for more members. I also dedicate this story to the community I live in who continually give with generous hearts, open hands, and a true volunteer spirit.

Lastly, I want to say thank you to Nancy and Caroline at Melange Publishing, for believing in me.

Dear Diary,

It's been a year now, and I still feel her loss every day. She's my first thought when I wake and my last thought when my head hits the pillow. If I'm lucky, she shows up in my dreams, sitting on the end of a couch and smiling her infectious grin. Her blue eyes sparkle as she chatters away. When I wake and find her gone, it's a harsh reality.

The days we were close seem so far away now. Some days they feel like dreams, but I know they were real. I've tried to go to church, and I'll keep trying, for our parents, but it's hard. I know it is where we find healing, but it's also where I feel the most broken. Everyone has their sorrows and struggles, and I'm not the only one; but her loss is overwhelming. It's like there's a hole inside me that will never be filled.

I try to keep going, in honor of my sister's memory, as she was always a doer and a fighter, and she wouldn't want me to give up. She's the reason I started going to the L. J. Youth Center. Although I've only been volunteering there a few weeks, I think I can do some good. I love meeting all the kids and listening to their struggles. They remind me of her stories and the kids she taught. It feels good to be able to help someone else with my ability to show up.

Goal: Today I will be present.

Maria

Chapter One

I stumble into the kitchen and interrupt an elderly make-out session at the kitchen sink. Awk-ward. There's a high-pitched ringing in the room that only I seem to hear. A wrinkled hand hiding in the back of Dale's shirt darts out and snatches the offending hearing aid from his ear. The ringing becomes shriller as she hands it to me.

"Turn that confounded thing off, will ya?" Daisy shouts at me, even though I'm standing less than two feet away.

I fiddle with the dial and turn it down. The ringing stops. "Here, Dale."

He gives me a wink as he puts his hearing aid back in place. He pats Daisy's jegging-clad camouflage butt as he moseys over to the coffeepot. "Thanks, Darlin'."

I laugh. "I ain't your darlin', don't you think one woman is enough?"

"I s'pose, but I ain't gettin' any younger, and I've got plenty of love to go around." Dale gives me his signature wink beneath his black cowboy hat he dons the minute his size 11 feet hit the floor.

"Just keep up your jawin' Dale." Daisy gives him a glare. "This house has plenty of other beds to sleep in."

Dale chuckles. "Aw, honey. Wouldn't be the first time I've been kicked out of bed, and I'm sure it won't be the last."

I grab my coffee and apple and head out the front door. Five minutes later, I'm scanning my ID badge at the front door of The Golden Ages, the long-term care facility that feels like my second home. The twelve-hour workday passes quickly as I count medications, train new floor nurses, do assessments, and fill out the daily paperwork. Before I know it, my shift is over and I'm back at the house. I open the front door that leads to the kitchen, bathroom, and downstairs. I love the layout of the house. Smells of dinner welcome me as I enter the kitchen, and I can't help but wonder why I didn't say yes to this setup sooner.

The state of Texas is trying something new by following the progressive example of a similar setup originating in other countries. Young people live with the elderly and they work together to meet each other's financial and emotional needs. My elderly friend and roommate, Daisy, loves to remind me often of what a Godsend I am to her and her husband Dale; but most of the time I think it's the other way around. In this valley town of around 30,000 people that has a state college, junior college, and a technical college, it's not hard to find young singles looking for rentals. After living for a year with the moodiest drama mama I've ever known, I was more than relieved to find a little normalcy with Daisy and Dale.

The dinner bell rings loud from the porch, a carry-over of Dale's ranching days. We meander to the kitchen and sit down to gather at the table. I'm comforted by Daisy's soft, wrinkled hand gripping mine while Dale and I bow our heads. Daisy knocks Dale's big black hat from his head before she prays.

"Dear Lord, thank you for another day of this wonderful life you've seen fit to give us. Thank you for bringing sweet Maria into our lives. Lord, please heal her broken heart." She gives my hand an extra squeeze. "And help us to see others through your eyes, to serve with our hands, love with our hearts, and praise you with our mouths; that all will see You in each one of us here. Amen." Daisy and I lift our heads, but Dale's head full of white hair remains bowed.

"I said amen!" Daisy raises her voice at the reverent, hearing-impaired Dale. Her effort remains unrewarded, as she continues to stare a hole through the top of his bowed head.

I nudge his foot.

He lifts his head with a smile, puts his hands together, and looks heavenward. "Thanks for the grub, Lord. Let's eat," he growls in his gravelly voice. He leans over, picks up his hat and hangs it on the corner of his chair.

Daisy passes her famous creamy peas to me, and I swear I hear the wheels turning in her head as she zeroes in on me with a blue-eyed laser-beam stare. Her skin may be wrinkled, but her eyes haven't lost a bit of shine or sparkle.

"I've been praying on it, Maria. I think we need another roommate. Three's kind of an awkward number. It'd sure be nice to have a young man around. Dale's getting up in years, and he can't clean the gutters or fix the plumbing, what with his arthritis."

I sigh, as this really isn't a 'new' idea. "Daisy. I can clean the gutters. I know how to climb a ladder."

Daisy slaps the table. "Maria! Get off your high horse with all your women's lib ideas! Let a man be a man and climb his darn ladder! Just because you can climb on a roof doesn't mean you should!"

I take a deep breath and mentally count to ten. "Daisy, we've talked about this before. You're not doing any matchmaking with me." I look down at my plate and try to focus. "I'm not ready yet." I wink at Dale. "Besides, I enjoy my roof-walking. It makes me feel like I'm living on the edge."

"Maria. It's been a year since you lost your sister. You need to get out more. It's not healthy for someone your age to live between work and home."

Daisy's words shame me. I know Liz wouldn't want me sitting at home, moping, but I can't help it. I miss her, and it makes me sad to think about how many years she could have had.

Daisy slides her gaze away from me, a telltale sign of stretching the truth. "You give me too much credit. I'm not trying to be a matchmaker!"

"You're not?" I can't help but rib her. "Are you sure? I recall a want ad you put out a few months back, offering free rent for *six* months. Do you remember the tools that showed up for that deal? You've got to be careful, Daisy. You can't trust just anyone."

"I remember," Dale chimes in, laughing out loud. "I remember. There were some real knuckleheads!"

"See, Daisy." I wave a hand in Dale's direction. "We're doing just fine! Besides, we just got into a groove. Things are running smoothly, and I'm not ready for a change."

Daisy shakes her head back and forth. "I don't like you two ganging up on me. And I'm careful! That's why I've been *prayin'* on it! The Lord will answer my prayers, just you wait and see. The right person will come along."

I roll my eyes as I take another delicious bite of supper. "What makes you think the Lord has any interest in my love life, or the lack of one?"

Daisy grabs my wrist. Her fingernails dig in. "The Lord wants you to be happy, Maria. Are you happy?"

Her question cuts me to the bone. "Daisy, don't you have a filter? Let me enjoy my supper." I lay down my fork in frustration. "I'm trying to be happy. Isn't that good enough? I get up every day and I go to work. I'm not lying around in bed drinking wine and eating bonbons. I'm twenty-two years old, I've barely started my career as a nurse, and my work keeps me plenty busy."

"Maria." Daisy's not done, as she pats my hand. "Those are all good things, but you're not getting any younger. Why, I got married when I was just nineteen. When you know, you know."

Dale answers from across the table. "And I was too young to know better."

"Don't listen to him." Daisy swats at him with her hand. "The man would've starved to death if he hadn't come straight from his momma's house to being married to me."

"I can make a pretty mean ham sandwich." Dale's not ready to give in to Daisy's protesting. He gives me another one of his signature winks.

I sigh. "Daisy, you got married in a day when women didn't work. They stayed home and had lots of babies. I'm not ready for any of that!" I shake my head and imagine a baby in my arms. My eyes water. I look for a distraction as I rummage through the fridge.

"Now look what you did. You chased her away." Dale growls at Daisy.

Great, now I'm the reason for another one of their squabbles, a word I didn't know before I moved in with the *Odd Couple*, a show I didn't watch until Dale started teaching me every card game he knows in front of the T.V., and he knows plenty.

I walk back to the table holding salad dressing, even though we have no salad. I sit down and set it by my plate. Daisy raises a questioning eyebrow but says nothing.

Dale, ever the sweetheart, takes the salad dressing and pours some on his green beans.

"Dale! I've never seen you eat Ranch dressing on your beans," Daisy starts up again.

"Woman!" He gives her a stubborn look. "I'll eat Ranch if I want. Stay outta my plate!"

Daisy turns back to me. I try to hold up under her

measuring stare. "What's this about you lying around in your bed? You're made of sterner stuff than that."

"How would you know?" Her barbs feel like hot irons in my side. "You've only known me for two months. How do you know what I'm made of?"

"I know more than you think." Daisy grins. "I found some pretty interesting reading when I was straightening your room the other day."

No freaking way. "You read my diary?"

Dale lays down his fork. "We both read it, and I gotta say, Maria, I had no idea you have so much emotion. It made my soul feel good. I thought all the youth today are pretty desensitized. I was relieved to find out you've been going to the L. J. Youth Center. Daisy and I were beginning to think you'd turned to liquor or worse with all that depression."

I want to sink under the table, but I'm too angry. "I can't believe you two! You had no business reading through my diary when I was at work."

Daisy's eyes get wide. She doesn't look the least bit sorry! "Oh, give me a break. You're locked up tighter than Fort Knox. I can't help you if you won't talk to me. Besides, what else have I got to do all day? I'm too old to work. I can't knit anymore. My arthritic hands won't let me. I'm not made for watching soaps all day on the tellie. Dale's no use for entertainment when he sleeps half the day, and there's only so many books this old woman can read."

"Alright, alright." Now I feel bad. "The next time I go to the L. J. Youth Center, you can go with me, but it's all volunteer work. I'm not in it for the pay. We do a lot of sorting donations and folding clothes. The reward is I get to meet some really great kids."

"Wait a minute!" Daisy's eyes get all fiery. "Is that the place where the kids serve community service? I mean, shouldn't they be in juvie? You sure you want to spend your spare time with criminals?"

"Daisy! They're not bad kids. They just need guidance. Most of them don't have much, if any, support at home. They need answers. They just don't know where to look. We help each other. Don't come if you don't want to."

She shakes her head. "I didn't say I wasn't coming, but they better not be packing."

"Packing?" I give a snort. "Packing—Daisy? Where'd you learn that phrase?"

Daisy's chin lifts a little. "I watch the cop shows. I know the language. Anyway…after dinner, would you be a dear and check out the basement bathroom? Dale thinks there's a leak in the back corner."

"Sure." I head to my room downstairs to turn on Netflix for a bit and zone out. It's hard to believe Christmas is a little over a month away. There's not a single part of me that wants to put up a tree or hang Christmas lights.

Soon enough, my laptop is lit up with men on horses and I get lost in the story and lose a few hours. On the screen, guns are a blazin' as they run at each other across an open field.

Dale's gravelly voice cuts into my Hollywood moment. "That's bold talk for a one-eyed fat man…" Jeff Bridges lies on the ground, about to meet his death, but then a shot rings out from Matt Damon's shotgun. "The Texas Rangers..they don't make 'em like they used to."

I laugh at Dale's comment. "Do you really believe that? Surely there's some honest men left in this world."

"I 'spose so, darlin', but they're getting fewer and far between." He clears his throat and smacks his forehead. "Ahh, you've got someone waitin' on ya. She showed up on the doorstep. Daisy's all lathered up."

Chapter Two

I can't make heads or tails of what Dale just said. I climb out of my blanket nest and glance at the night sky through my curtains, muttering. "It's dark out. I wonder who would be stopping by this late."

I follow Dale upstairs. I walk slowly behind him.

"Heck if I know. Come take a look see." Dale's got better hearing than he lets on. I bite my tongue as he answers my muttering.

I shuffle into the kitchen and look towards the front door; but Daisy sitting at the kitchen table catches my eye. I turn towards her, confused. Why is there an infant car seat on the table? What in the world? I scan all that I can see, but don't see any other adults.

"Come here." Daisy mouth whispers to me from across the room. Her eyes are wet with tears. She clutches a shaking paper in her outstretched hand as her other hand rises to her lips. "Shhh."

I walk towards Daisy. I'm not sure what to make of all this. When the car seat moves a breadth of an inch, I almost shriek out loud before I manage to stop myself. The cutest hand I've ever seen pops out, and the tiniest of fingers stretches, as if startled. I hear a faint exhaling as the hand disappears. My heel walk turns to tiptoes as I rush to stand behind Daisy, as if she can protect me from this helpless little stranger who has disrupted our unencumbered lives. I glance down at the baby sleeping undisturbed and unaware in her little car seat, the only home she has left. A small, dark curl peeks out from her pink-and-blue striped hat that stretches around her head; all of its elastic worn thin. My wooden heart shatters and starts to bleed.

I snatch the offending letter from Daisy's shaking hand and leave the room, not wanting to read its contents in front of the innocent baby.

Dear Maria,

I'm not much a praying person, but I don't know what else to do. I've been searching and praying for an Angel to care for my Joy, and I think you could be what she needs. I've lived off others so long, I guess I know how to find vulnerability. Forgive me for leaving my burden with you, but I know you'll do right by her. I've watched you at work and with the kids at the center. I know you know how to love.

I've been sad for a long time, and I thought the gift of my Joy would take away my sadness, but this sickness inside is too much for me to handle. I'm not a fit mother, and I feel my end is near. The choices I've made are going to catch up with me soon. Joy deserves more than I can give her. Please don't look for me, I learned a long time ago how to be invisible. If all you remember about me is Joy; well, she's the best part of me.

There was a man, Nick Laus. He doesn't know about Joy. I only met him the one time. He's not a bad man. He was just another vulnerable person I came across. Please take care of my Joy. She deserves all the love you can give her.

A grateful, lost mother

I read this letter over and over, and my panic grows. What do I do? I glance back at the empty kitchen, save for the car seat. I rush in her direction. I pause when I hear Dale and Daisy's voices carry up the long hallway.

"You can't keep her, Daisy. We've got to take her to the cops." My harried footsteps carry me down the hallway, and my actions surprise me as I reach out to Dale to get his attention.

"You're not taking her anywhere. I've got a name. I'll take a few days off and look the guy up. Joy deserves that at least." The firmness in my voice surprises me as I look up at Dale. It's like my mother has taken over my body, and her voice is spilling out.

"I don't like this." Dale turns to me and crosses his arms across his chest. "I don't like this. The longer she's in the house, the more the two of you will get attached. And what if the cops show up? You could be charged with kidnapping!"

"Oh Dale. Relax." Daisy pats his hand. "You've been watching too many 48 hours. We didn't kidnap her. She showed up here. We couldn't just leave her outside to freeze to death. I think you're just worried you won't get my attention anymore. Baby Joy needs our help."

"Hmph." Dale isn't appeased. "Don't tell me to relax. I didn't *ask f*or a baby to be dropped on my doorstep! I really don't like this."

Daisy cocks her head to the side. "Dale. Why don't you go back to watching your program? Just pretend she's not here. Go on. Shoo." She turns to me. "Come on, Maria. Let's go google Nick."

Dale shakes his head and goes to his room, calling over his shoulder, "I'm not sittin' out here. I won't be a witness to any more of this nonsense. Y'all are in for a late night; better make yourselves some coffee."

I follow Daisy back to the kitchen.

"Now, the first thing we need is a crib. That car seat isn't a proper bed for her. And, formula, baby food, and diapers. Maria, you'd better make a Dollar General run."

I look away with a smile. She's already in grandma-mode, barking out orders left and right. Thank goodness, because I have no clue.

My mind is so muddled, I can't think straight. I grab a notepad from the kitchen drawer and scribble the items down furiously. I pause for half a second and look Daisy in the eye. "Thank you, Daisy. What would I do if you weren't here?"

"I guess you'd figure it out." Daisy chuckles. "But I'm here now. Get on with it, then. Better hurry before she wakes. Oh, and grab a few bottles." Daisy holds her tiny, wrinkled hand to her brow and shakes her head. "Dear Lord, help us do right by this little one."

I tear out the front door with my list and race down the street to the store on the corner. My heart races in my chest. What am I doing dashing through store aisles buying baby supplies? My hands tremble, and I almost drop my shopping basket. The cashier rings me up.

"That'll be $75.00, miss."

I shake my head in disbelief and mutter, "Babies are expensive." I stare at the cashier, who looks back at me like I've lost my mind. I hurriedly grab up the sacks and throw them in the back of my Honda Fit. Suddenly, it feels like it's not big enough to be safe. I'm going to need something much larger and heavier to protect precious baby Joy.

I pull back into the drive. A new tiredness takes over me. My days of living simply are gone. The contents of these bags feel like a thousand pounds as I walk up the front porch steps. I pause for a minute with uncertainty. I take a calming breath and step forward. I'm leaving my old life behind. I'm a mom now. I step determinedly towards a new and exciting future and feel a little lighter as I open the door.

I step around the corner to the kitchen. Daisy sits as still as can be while she watches over baby Joy. She looks at me questioningly. "Where's the crib?"

I drop the bags to the floor with a clatter. I slap my forehead. Joy's cry fills the air. "Oh shoot. I knew I forgot something!"

Daisy laughs. "That's the first step to becoming a new mother. Forgetfulness!"

I watch with envy as Daisy has Joy out of the car seat in seconds. She lifts her to her shoulder with ease, sways around the room, and shushes her. As Joy's big dark eyes fix on me, a possessiveness I don't understand enters my body. As sure as I live and breathe, Joy belongs with me now. I'm mesmerized. The spell breaks as Daisy exits the kitchen. She dances and hums around the living room, and pats Joy's bum as Joy lightly bumps against her shoulder, fussing quietly. Joy's dark eyes look all around.

"Now that you're back, get out a can of formula and make Joy a bottle, but don't make it too warm," Daisy whispers to me.

Daisy may as well be speaking Greek. I have no clue what I'm doing. I rummage around in the bags, grab the can of formula, and frantically hold it up under the light over the kitchen sink. I read the instructions and use my phone to google the right temperature for a baby's bottle. Somehow, I manage to put the bottle together.

Daisy wanders over with a fussy Joy. "Oh, for heaven's sake, take the bottle and tip it to spill a drop on your wrist. That's how you gage the temperature. Didn't they teach you anything in nursing school?" Daisy's words of wisdom singe my ears.

I ignore her smart remark and try to do what I'm told. I hand the bottle to Daisy, but I'm unable to keep my big mouth shut. "My wrist says it's lukewarm."

Daisy gives me a nod of approval. She takes the bottle and sits down in the recliner. I smile at Joy's greedy little hands reaching for the bottle. She closes her eyes as if to shut out her surroundings before settling herself into Daisy's side, quickly draining it. She drops the bottle to the floor and sticks her thumb in her mouth. Daisy shifts in her chair before looking up at me. "Maria, you're going to have to take her. My arthritis is acting up again. I can't sit here much longer with her."

Immediately I panic. "What? I don't… I can't."

"You can." By the look on her face, Daisy's having none of my excuses. "Just don't be nervous. If you're nervous, she'll feel it, and you'll upset her."

"Daisy. I don't know how to hold a baby."

"Well, then it's time you learn. Just do what comes naturally. Now get down here and get her before I drop her on the floor."

I drop to my knees, and Daisy hands her over. Joy feels just right as soon as we touch. I hold her close to me. Somehow, I knew this was what it would feel like. I don't care about Daisy's smug smile; I can't take my eyes off of Joy. She's absolutely perfect.

"Good night," I whisper. I nod to Daisy. I don't want to startle Joy.

I pad softly down the hallway with Joy until I get to my room where I lay a sleepy baby down in my blanket nest, being careful not to bump her as I lay down opposite her. She wiggles around until she's snuggled into my side. Suddenly, I'm drowning in emotions, and I start to weep. I weep tears for the parts of me I didn't know were missing, and for the hand Joy's been dealt. I've been trying to find purpose, but I think it's found me.

Chapter Three

I wake to find myself all alone, and panic sets in. I jump out of bed and look all around the floor, as if I'm going to find a baby there. There's a soft knocking on my door.

"Wake up, darlin'. The little miss has been up for a while." Dale's voice sneaks into my room. I throw on a hoodie over my tank. I shuffle out to the kitchen, thankful for my flannel sleep pants, as the cool November air seeps in under the front door.

My eyes scan the room. "Where's Daisy?"

Dale has an ornery grin. "She 'bout wore herself out last night with all the baby excitement."

"Oh. Well, how'd you get baby Joy then?"

He looks at the floor and slides his foot back and forth. "I thought I heard some fussin' around when I walked by your door, so I came and got her. You were dead to the world."

Now I feel guilty. "Why didn't you wake me up?"

"Pshaw." Dale chuckles. "Me and the little miss been gettin' acquainted. She kinda likes my warblin'."

I'm suspicious. "You heard Joy fussing…through my door…yet you can't hear Daisy when she's yelling 'Grace' across the table?"

Dale gives me a shy grin. "Selective hearing, I guess."

"You scoundrel." I can't help but chuckle at his antics. "Selective hearing my butt."

"Daisy loves it." Dale gives me a big smile. He looks so comfortable with Joy.

"Dale. How do you know, I mean, I didn't know you like babies. It's just, you seem at ease with her."

"Now, don't go gettin' all soft on me, darlin'. I didn' say I like babies, but I know what to do with 'em. I'm an older brother, you know, and a dad, and a grandpa…"

I feel silly. "That's true…well, thanks."

His eyes light up. "So, when you going to google this Nick?"

"Thanks for the reminder." Dang it, he remembers. "I'll go and fetch my laptop." My google search is not too productive until I get to Facebook, and Bingo! Great. I look over at Dale. "It looks like he's an Army guy, and his base is about five hours from here, one state over. That'd be too easy if this is the guy I'm looking for." I tear my eyes from the screen, but it's hard. There's something about the guy's smile that holds me captive. I just want to keep staring. Maybe I should keep my distance and call him on the phone. I look over at Joy. Her eyes are wide open and full of wonder. She needs to know who her father is, and I won't know unless I meet him in person.

"Well, what're you waitin' for?" Dale paces back and forth and hums to Joy. He leans over my shoulder slightly. He peeks at the screen. "You going to Snapchat him, or whatever it is you young people do these days? Strangers meet each other in a virtual world and then they wonder how they end up robbed or in pieces in a trash can…"

"Dale." I look up at him from my chair. "Settle down. I'm not doing any of that. I…I think I'll meet him in person. I need to look him in the eye."

Dale muses this idea over in his head. "Yeah, that'd be better."

Daisy sneaks up behind me. She leans over my shoulder, and I smell her flowery perfume. “Is that your guy? He’s easy on the eyes.”

“What?” I hate that I’m blushing. “I hadn’t noticed, and he’s not my guy. I’m just trying to help Joy.”

She laughs and smacks me lightly me on the shoulder. “If you meet a handsome fellar, what’s so wrong with that?”

I concede her point. “He’s not bad looking, that’s true.”

She smacks me on the shoulder again. “The man is gorgeous, Maria. Open your eyes.”

There’s a little grunt from Dale holding Joy in the corner. “I’ll try not to take offense at that, darlin’. Quit eye ballin’ the man in the computer. I’m right here.”

Daisy sidles up to Dale, who stands by the sink. She pats one side of his chest. “Don’t worry, old man. You know you’ve *got me*. I’m just enjoyin’ the scenery. Now hand me that bottle and the baby. I think precious Joy’s still hungry.”

“Daisy.” Dale looks down at her. “She’s not hungry. She’s just bored. I already fed her.” Dale sets the mostly empty bottle down and walks into the living room by the big picture window. He holds Joy away from him and speaks to her in low tones about what’s outside.

“Maria.” Daisy clears her throat. “I’ve been thinking, Maria. The weekend just started, and this is the first day of your four days off. Now would be a good time as ever to go find this soldier, especially with Veteran’s Day so close. I bet it’ll make him easier to locate. Plus, you don’t have time to spare. This is kind of a sticky situation. Something about today just feels like perfect timing for you to go on your search. Dale and I can take care of little Joy while you’re gone.”

“Are you sure, Daisy?”

“Maria.” Daisy laughs at me! “I raised five of my own plus a few extras on the weekends here and there. I think I can handle one baby.”

My heart lurches, and I fight panic. Things feel like they’re moving way too fast. I run back to my room to grab my phone charger, jacket, and hat. I head for the door, and Dale hands me a paper lunch bag. “I put a banana and a sandwich in there for the road. And here’s a few bottles of water.”

I give him a quick squeeze and a hug, surprising myself. “Thanks, Dale!”

Questions race through my mind as I drive along the highway. My head spins. Despite driving five hours, I’m full of apprehension and jangling nerves as I drive onto the army base.

Chapter Four

I've never been to an army base before. I pull up to what I hope is the main office, feeling strange and uncertain as I see men in fatigues wandering around. I enter the double doors and head straight for the middle desk, where a rather severe-looking young man sits.

"May I help you, ma'am?"

"Um." I clear my throat and speak up. "Yes. I'm, I'm looking for Nick Laus."

He looks directly at me and hesitates a few agonizing moments, as if I'm hanging on his every word. "I'm sorry, ma'am. He's retired and lives as a civilian. He's not here."

"I see." I've hit an unwelcome roadblock, but I'm determined. "Well, I can't imagine why he didn't give the army his new address. Where did he move to?"

He looks offended. "We cannot give you his forwarding information. It's classified."

I'm not giving up that easily. "Well, what I have to tell him is very important, and time sensitive. I would really appreciate it if you would reconsider." I try my best to look desperate but earnest at the same time.

"Ma'am." He stands up, crosses his arms on his chest, and moves his feet farther apart. A power stance. *Oh boy.* "This is the U.S. army. We take the rules quite seriously. I don't just give private, confidential, information out to every woman who sashays in here with a sad look on her face."

This man is highly annoying. I turn away from him to face the other direction and focus on breathing deep before I say something I'll regret. When I think I've got myself under control, I turn around to see if by some small miracle, the man has changed his mind. Nope. He looks as determined as ever to maintain his position of power from behind the desk.

I'm ticked. "Okay. Well, thank you so much for not helping me." I stand here a second later, and try to stare the man-boy down, as if that's going to cause him to give up the information. It doesn't. He stares unflinchingly back.

There's movement in the corner of my eye as a guy hops up from a bench. He's so still and quiet, I'm not sure how long he was there, which is hard to believe, as he's all tall, blond, and chiseled. He walks up in his gym shorts and a ripped tee with a sweat spot that's still growing. He knocks hard on the desk and pulls up so close I get a whiff of his manliness. This makes me a little uncomfortable, which I think is his intention.

He leans over the desk and gets right in the guy's face. "Maley! Don't be such a hardass," Mr. blond and beautiful barks.

I can't help but giggle, but he just keeps going.

"There's no yellow line over here. Don't go all postal worker on her now." He turns to me with a smile so unexpected, my giggling ceases and my skin starts to tingle as he looks me up and down and gives a low whistle. *What a hound dog.* He turns back to the red-faced man standing behind the desk. "She looks pretty harmless to me." He waits a few seconds and stares hard at Maley, whose face is turns beet red, while his lips remained pursed in a thin red line. "Not going to give it up, huh? Well. Suit yourself, soldier." He side eyes me and winks! "Keep fighting danger," he replies in a resigned Owen Wilson voice. "From behind your small plastic desk." He gives it a hard knock as if to test its sturdiness. He turns back to me again, all smiles and charm. "The only thing you're in danger of darlin'…is stoppin' traffic."

"Boy." I can't help it. I laugh out loud. "You're just full of…something…"

He gives me a wink and takes my elbow. "C'mon darlin'. What say you and I take a little stroll…" As soon as we get outside, he drops a little of his swagger and sobers right up. He's all intense as he stares me down. "So. What is the nature of your inquiry of Nick?"

What? "Inquiry? Are you some sort of detective? And where'd your home-on-the-range accent go?"

He grins at me again, and I just about lose my train of thought. This man's smile should be outlawed. "I just like to mess with the desk boy and get under his skin. I's just havin' a little fun with him. So! What do you want with my friend, Nick?"

I'm not sure what to say. "I'm um, I'm afraid my inquiry is a little delicate and personal, and not your business."

His gaze flies to my stomach, and my hand goes there, a natural act of defense. He clears his throat, takes my elbow again, and steers me farther away from the front of the building.

"Just what do you think you are doing, manhandling me?"

He leans down in my space. His breath touches my ear. "I figger our conversation doesn't need to be done in front of the guys," he whispers.

I lean back and try to move away, but he still has my elbow. "Who says I'm talking to you anymore? I think I said all I'm going to say."

"Well, how bad do you want to find Nick?" He releases my

arm. "I know where he is, but I'm not telling you anything unless you tell me why you're looking for him."

This guy may be smoking hot, but he's kind of annoying. "What are you, his guardian? You haven't even told me your name yet. Besides, he looks perfectly capable of taking care of himself."

He looks at me like I'm suspect. "My name is Thomas. I'm Nick's best friend, and I want to know why you're after him. Are you trying to baby-trap him? I know for a fact Nick can't be your baby daddy. We've been on the same deployment for the past ten months. It was his last assignment before his retirement."

I'm tired of this dance. I really need the address. "I'm not pregnant, but, um. There is a baby. She's six months old. Please tell me where he is. I'm trying to do the right thing here."

His eyes revert back to flirt mode. This guy is something else. "So you're not off the market?"

I can't help it. "What am I, a pig?"

He throws his head back with laughter. "Whooeee. You're a feisty one." He raises his eyebrows in ponderous silence as he rocks back on his heels and gets all serious. "Would you be interested in having a drink with me?"

I can't believe what I'm saying, as this guy's really funny, and not at all hard to look at. "Thank you, but no. I'm not looking for a relationship right now. My life kind of became more complicated overnight, and I don't need any more distractions."

He throws up his hands and gives me an incorrigible look. I can't help but forgive him.

"Hey, can't blame a guy for trying. We Army guys don't have a lot of time to be subtle. We tend to be more forward and get right to the point—hazards of the job, I guess. Let me see your phone." He holds out his hand.

"What? Why?"

"Relax, lady. I'm givin' you Nick's address. It shouldn't take you long. It's not too far from here, but there's a lot of side streets and turns. The easiest thing would be to GPS it."

I reluctantly hand my phone over. "Thank you. I really appreciate it."

"Happy to help." He laughs. "Just wish I was there to see the fireworks. Nick's head's gonna explode."

Chapter Five

No sooner am I in the car, then Daisy calls. "Have you met him yet?"

"Um, no." I tap the wheel in irritation. "Apparently, he's retired from the army already. He must be older than I thought."

"Well, maybe not. Maybe he joined when he was sixteen or something, you know, like the ROTC program."

"Yeah, maybe." I start up the car, back out, and follow my GPS directions.

Daisy's' not done. "The fact that he stayed in the army so long speaks for his character and shows commitment. That's important."

"Okay, okay, Daisy. Don't get all excited. He's probably married." I stop. Why didn't I think of that before now? "Oh, no. What if he's married? Thomas didn't say."

"Who's Thomas?"

"He's Nick's best friend. He gave me Nick's address. Daisy, what if he has other children? This will upset everything!"

"Calm down, Maria. If he had a family, don't you think Thomas would have told you? I didn't see any pictures of women or children on his Facebook profile. You're getting all worried about things that may not even exist. Don't go borrowing trouble. You're trying to find reasons not to see him. You drove all the way there. You can't back out now."

"I didn't say I was backing out." My stomach churns. "I'm just considering all the possibilities." Like the fact that he's retired military, probably fifty-plus years old with the disposition of a Kodiak bear since he's never been married. Or maybe he's a gun nut who fishes all day and drinks a six-pack every night because he prefers to be alone.

"Maria. I have a good feeling about this. I really do." That makes one of us.

"Daisy. Stop thinking about his looks, they're messing with your good judgment. That might not even be his picture. People do that, you know. They catfish and use some random picture to lure in their victims." I close my mouth. I have to stop, or I will freak myself out, and then I'll turn this car around and go right back home.

"He has kind eyes. That's definitely a good sign." It's like I'm talking to myself, as Daisy just keeps going.

I come to a stop. "I'm not arguing with you anymore right now, Daisy. I give up. GPS says I'm here. I'll talk to you later."

The first thing I see as I pull up is a huge black truck. I hop out and head for the front door before I lose my nerve. I ring the doorbell but get no response. Music floats up from the backyard. I follow it. Bruno Mars blares in my ears, but the sounds fade when I see the man lying on the bench. He grunts a little as he lifts the bar. Holy guacamole. I could take a bite out of that bulging bicep. I shake my head to clear my crazy thoughts as I approach. I cast a shadow on the ground. The man sits up. Have mercy. Mark Consuelos and Justin Baldoni have nothin' on this guy. I hope my mouth is still closed.

Focus, Maria, focus. Look at something else...suddenly the pair of hedge clippers hanging on his garage wall is quite fascinating. Crap balls. I hadn't planned on losing my cool so fast, but his chest is so bare, and he's so sweaty. This garage feels way too small. I turn sideways and scan his yard in self-defense. Movement catches the side of my eye. The music stops.

"May I help you?"

I'm in serious trouble. His deep, sexy voice matches the rest of him. I could listen to it all day. I glance his direction for a second in acknowledgment before turning back to look out at his yard. "Um, yes. I know you don't know me, but I, uh, well I received a letter from a stranger, and your name was in it."

"Okay…well what did the letter say?"

I'm nervous. I fidget terribly, but I can't seem to stand still as I dig my fingernails into my fisted hands and rock back on my heels. "Well, it, uh, it's about something that may belong to you, I'm just not sure."

"Can you turn and face me, or am I going to have a conversation with the side of you?"

I turn slightly; just enough to see he's still shirtless. "Could you, just, well put a shirt on please?" I hate that my voice just squeaked.

He stands up from his bench and walks past me. He's so close his arm brushes mine as he passes. There's the slightest bit of hesitation, so minute, I almost think I imagine it. Nope. Now he's stopped right in front of me. He reaches up to scratch his neck and gives me a chance to see that scrumptious bicep even closer and smell all his manly sweat. Why doesn't any of this turn me off? I take a deep breath in to calm myself and try to focus on something nonsexual, like his eardrum. But he's so tall and so close! All I can see is the rivulet of sweat that flows down his earlobe; hesitating before it falls to his perfectly formed clavicle, leading to his beautiful pecs. I've officially been caught staring…way too long…my gaze shoots to the ground. I've got to get a grip and escape this all-consuming lust. There's a throat clearing somewhere in the distance. I look up and find myself staring into the darkest eyes I've ever seen, and yet somehow they twinkle. He looks exactly like his picture.

"I had to scratch an itch…" he says as his eyes roam over my body.

The man's as smooth as butter, and I'd love a little taste, but I'm on a mission, so I try as hard as I can to pretend this man is a resistant patient and turn on my no-nonsense nurse voice. "I'd like to speak with you inside please, or at least somewhere we can both sit down."

"So." He sighs. "This visit is all business, huh? Nothing else?"

"Unbelievable." Boy, he's pushing my buttons. "You've just met me! And already, you're hitting on me. You don't even know why I'm here. I could be…I could be serving some sort of legal papers."

"This is true." Anger flashes in his eyes briefly. "Are you?"

I get lost in his lips and try in vain to reorient. "Am I what?"

His intense focus and unblinking stare beneath those sinfully dark lashes is unnerving. "Are you here to serve me an official court document?"

"Were you expecting one?"

"No." His posture relaxes slightly. "Not that I'm aware of."

His good looks are too distracting.

"Then why would you ask that?"

"You're the one who started that conversation! Plus, you just seem so serious, and so… uptight. So I just thought…"

"You thought nothing!" Good! Let him think I'm a nun! "You don't strike me as the kind of guy who plans too far ahead. Anyway, I'm not from the court. I'm here of my own volition. I just came by to see what kind of guy you are, and because I felt obligated."

His face falls and his eyes narrow. "Why would it matter what kind of guy I am? And who says you are any judge of character?"

"Please." His voice has gotten louder, so I lean in and grab his arm. Heat burns through me and I look down, half expecting to see cinders falling to the ground. I jerk my head up and look into his eyes. I feel foolish. "I really don't want to stand outside and hash these things out in front of the neighbors."

"Boy, you really want to come in my house." He gives me a suggestive wink and wheels around. He marches away from me as he heads towards the house.

I hate that my eyes are glued to his backside as he walks away. The man can really fill out a pair of shorts. I try to look elsewhere, and only get as far as his calves. This is ridiculous. I have a goal. I need to stick to it. I follow him inside. I note it's very tidy, and the kitchen smells wonderful. Without thinking, I go to the crockpot and sneak a peek.

He returns to the kitchen wearing a tank, which doesn't do much to cover all that golden brown skin. His eyebrow goes up, as I'm caught snooping in his next meal.

"Make yourself at home, don't mind me."

I almost drop the lid before setting it down carefully. "I'm sorry. I was just, um, curious. It smelled so good. Your girlfriend must be a very good cook."

"What makes you think there's someone else? You think I can't cook?"

Yes. "Um, no." I cough. "I think if I open my mouth a little wider, I can fit my whole foot in." I shoot him a small smile.

He grins and ducks his head. "Okay, that was kind of cute."

I clear my throat again. "It's just, I'd rather know if you have a significant other before I go any farther with this conversation."

"Oh?" His lips quirk up at one end. He gives me a flirtatious smile as he comes closer. "And why would that be?"

I wave my hands in front of me. "Stop."

He stops moving and puts his hands up in surrender. "Easy, there. I'm not going to hurt you."

"I… I know that. But, you might want to sit down for what I've got to say."

He sits down and takes up half the couch. His long hairy legs stretch out in front of him. He throws his arm over the back. He looks up at me. "Well?"

"Oh, right. Well, there's no easy way to say this, so I guess I'll just say it. It involves a baby."

He sits straight up and leans forward. His elbows rest on his knees as his hands open wide. His fingertips bump into each other repeatedly. He peers up at me through his black/brown eyes with eyelashes so long and curly, I'm envious. He's really messing with my concentration. "I see. Are you like some sort of attorney?"

"No." I laugh a little. "No. The baby…the baby is with me. I mean, she's at home. My friends are watching her, while I get this sorted out, but I'm taking care of her."

He's still leaning over. He lifts his head again and tilts his head to the side as he looks up. "So, *I'm* what you have to sort out? Is that what you're saying?" He studies me just long enough to make me squirm. "I'm guessing you're not her mother, or else you wouldn't talk about her as her caregiver."

"Yes." This guy is quick. "Yes. That's true."

He looks me up and down and makes me feel all warm inside. "That makes more sense. I mean, I think I'd remember if we had…well if we'd been together."

What a thing to say! I can't believe this guy. It's like testosterone pours out of every cell in his body, and not in a good way. "I sure hope so. You're not the type of guy who doesn't remember someone the next morning, are you? Because that's just not going to work for me."

His expression changes to irritation. "Hold up. You're thinking I'm the father, but you're making the decisions on what acceptable behavior is? I mean, if I'm the father, and you're not her mother, well, what does it matter what you think?"

I hate that he has a good point, but I'm not about to admit that. "She entrusted me with her baby, so I have a say. I'm a person of my word, and my interest is what is best for Joy."

His chin juts out stubbornly. "Well, where is the mother? Why isn't she here?"

This is not a question I want to answer, but I don't know how to get out of answering it. "Um, I don't actually know."

"Come again?"

"I said I don't know, okay? I mean, this is all new to me. Joy kind of…kind of just showed up on my doorstep, but I don't want her going to just any stranger on the street. I have a responsibility to her now."

"So you just met this baby, and you're not met her mother, but you're here questioning me?"

He has a point, but I'm not about to tell him that. "Well, I didn't know what else to do. I mean, the mom wrote your name in her letter, and it's the only thing I had to go on."

"Where's the letter?" His eyes are narrowed again.

He doesn't believe me!

"Just a second." I dig it out of my back pocket. "Here." I slap it hard in his hand with too much satisfaction, but what do I look like? Some sicko that would take him on the Jerry Springer show for a paternity test?! I'm just trying to do the right thing.

I watch his face as he reads through the letter. I try to read his expression, but it remains the same. The silence stretches out over ten minutes. "Well, there's a chance I may not be the father of this child." He stares up at me.

"Yes." I try to make him understand. "Yes. I did read that, but I guess I figured I owed it to you to let you know. I mean, so you could make up your own mind."

"That's fair. Although now that I know, what kind of man

would I be if I just go on with my life, like this conversation never happened? I'm kind of in a precarious position."

The nerve of this man! "Well, I didn't exactly ask for a baby to be dropped on my porch, either. But here we are."

He studies me for a few very awkward, very long minutes. "Yes. Here we are. Would you…uh…would you like to stay for supper?"

"Um, okay." That's the last thing I expected. "Alright. I'd say I don't want to impose, but it's a little late for that. Thank you."

He hops up from the couch, all quick and graceful. "I usually spend supper time in front of the T.V. Do you watch *House Hunters*? It's the only show I DVR."

"That's fine. A new season starts tonight, if I remember correctly."

He puts a hand on my elbow. "Come in the kitchen, then. The plates are up in the cupboard over the microwave. Silverware's in the drawer right beneath it." There's a sense of intimacy I didn't expect as I join him in the living room. He mutes the T.V. and bows his head over his plate, saying a silent prayer of thanks. I do the same. The T.V. sound comes back on. We sit together and watch the couple hunting for their perfect house. Soon we're discussing the elements of the show. He points to the T.V. "That house would be perfect, except the backyard needs to be bigger."

I shake my head. "The backyard is fine, but the kitchen needs more space." I frown at him.

"The kitchen seemed fine to me." His voice is quiet but firm.

"No." This is kind of fun. "No. The kitchen is the heart of any home. It's where everybody gathers. Everyone knows that."

A commercial comes on. He turns to me. "Depends on the family. My family has most of their discussions in the living room in front of a football game." His gaze dances at me. He smirks. It's adorable.

I break eye contact first. "Well, my best memories happened at the supper table."

He gives me a killer grin. "Agree to disagree, then." We clink our Coca-Cola cans, and his pinkie brushes mine. His light touch goes all through me. I glance over at him. His face hasn't changed a bit. Great. This attraction appears to be one-sided.

He gets up during commercial and offers to take my plate. I follow him into the kitchen, and immediately regret it. He leans on the sink with his arms crossed across his chest. He pulls his snug tank even tighter, as if I need to see any more definition, as if the sight of his glistening bare chest earlier is not permanently etched in my memory. There's a smug grin on his face. He's enjoying my discomfort. My cheeks flame. I can feel it. There's nothing I can do to stop it, and I wish he'd quit staring.

Do I have something on my face? "What?!"

"I get to you, don't I?"

If you count wanting to kiss you until there's no tomorrow, then yes.

"No. It's not that. You're...you're just not what I expected." There, let him think about that!

"And what did you expect?" A fifty-year-old man with a beer gut and a nasty disposition.

I laugh a little. "I don't know, to be honest. I just...I just didn't expect who you are."

He's openly smirking. "Oh, and who am I?" Someone who makes me want everything – too much.

"Like you don't know how you look. I'm sure you've been given more than a few numbers when you go out." I hate this conversation. I'm sure he's eating it up.

"Sooo...you like how I look?"

Oh, my. Do you speak English? I stare hard at him.

"What difference does it make?" My back is up. "That's not...that's not what I'm here for. Excuse me, please. I need to rinse this dish." I sound like a nun in a classroom of misfits. My tone is as cold as Siberia.

He scoots over a hair and butts up against the sink.

I brush up against him and try to rinse the dish. He reaches out and toys with my ponytail and leans in to whisper in my ear. Holy hot tamales, I think I'm having a hot flash.

"So you're off limits? That's a shame."

I hate that I'm sighing, as I reach out to push against his chest, so he'll back off. My hand hits his rock-hard body and I'm frozen. All I can do is feel. My breathing becomes heavy. I yank my hand back like I've just touched a hot stove.

I wave my hands around like a madwoman. "I need some space. I'm just here for Joy. She's why I had to meet you. And now we've met. I think I'll go now. I'd like to come back tomorrow, if you have time. There's more we need to discuss. Please."

He steps away from me slowly. He hovers closer than I'd like. "If that's the case, why don't you stay here tonight?" He speaks all soft, and low, like I'm a skittish horse or something.

I back away from him and turn. I lean up against the sink with a fork in my hand. "I couldn't possibly stay here tonight. I barely know you! And did you not hear what I just said? I'm not here for any funny business. I'm here for Joy."

He grabs the fork from my hand. "Why don't you lay the weapon down." He smiles down at me. He turns sideways and palms the countertop. He pushes on it, flexes his biceps and breathes deep. I can't tell if he's showing off, or he's annoyed, but it's hot.

He looks over at me. His expression is all distant and polite. The guy can flip a switch. "I heard you. Loud and clear. But you still need a place to stay. I've got a spare room. Why waste your money on a hotel? Besides, do you really want to mess with trying to find a decent one this late in the day? I promise I'll behave." The grin he gives me turns my insides to mush, and I hate that I'm hoping a little that he'll renege on that promise.

"Well. It would be much simpler if I just stay here. As long as it's not too much of an imposition."

"It's fine. Really. It's just one night." His words are all innocent, and his tone is flippant, but the heat in his eyes says otherwise.

"At least let me wash your dishes." I turn my back on him again and start rinsing, trying to divert my thoughts from where they're headed every time I look at him. He pops up again, right behind my left ear. I feel his breath on my neck. His hand rests so soft on my hip, I almost don't feel it. Is he sniffing my hair?! I shake my head back and forth, and he moves back slightly, chuckling low.

"Nah. That's alright. I've got a dishwasher." He doesn't wait for me to move, as he reaches into the sink with both arms, brushes up both sides of me. His chest bumps against my back. I'm practically pinned to the sink as he slowly lifts his arms, a plate in each hand. I feel a chill as he backs away from me and turns to put the dishes in the dishwasher.

"Right, then. I'll just…I'll go find that spare room." I beat a retreat from the kitchen like it's on fire, taking deep breaths as I rush along blindly, wondering what I've gotten myself into. I'm halfway down a dark hallway, feeling my way along the dark paneled walls, when I hear his footsteps closing in on me. He's back. He tugs on my pants, pulling me backwards. He's got me by the back of my pants! I swat his hand away.

"Hold on there, slick. You're heading straight for my bedroom."

I'm all flustered. "Where's my room, then?!"

"Follow me." We head back the other direction. He opens a closed door and reaches in to turn on the light. "This is your room. It has its own bathroom too."

"Thank you. I'll go get my overnight stuff out of my car

then." I'm barely out the door of his house, and my phone rings. It's Daisy.

"Hey, Daisy. How's Joy? Is she doing okay?"

"Yes. No worries here. How's Nick?"

"Yummy. He's just as gorgeous in person as in his photo. It's perfectly awful. I mean, I can't keep my head around him."

"Well, you'll have to figure that one out on your own. The first time I met my Dale, my head was in the clouds for a whole week."

"Don't get excited, Daisy. It's not like that. He's just…he's just extremely good looking. Anyway, I'm staying at his place."

"What?! That's going kind of fast, isn't it?"

"No. I mean, he has a spare room, the one I'm sleeping in. It'll save me some time and money."

"Well, if you think you can resist temptation."

"Yes, Daisy. I'm pretty sure I can resist him. He's just eye candy. I need to get back inside. I'm in the car getting my overnight things."

"If you say so. Goodnight."

"Goodnight, give Joy a kiss for me."

"So long as you give Nick a kiss for me." She cackles in my ear. One minute she's scolding me for staying over, and the next she's encouraging me to steal a kiss! She's incorrigible.

"Daisy! I'm not here for that. Besides, I'm sure his kisses would quickly lead to something else! I'm not ready."

"Get off your high horse, Maria." She chuckles. "A kiss is pretty harmless. That's the fun of being young and single! Besides, haven't you heard about taking a test drive before you buy the vehicle?"

My ears burn. "He's not a car, he's a person."

"Same concept. You don't want to be with someone who doesn't get your motor revved up. That's all I'm saying."

"Daisy." I take a deep breath, wondering how Daisy sounds so much like my sister right now. "This is by far the weirdest and most awkward conversation I've ever had with you, and I'd like for it to end as soon as possible. Please."

There's cackling on the other end. "You're no fun. If that's what you want..."

"Goodbye, Daisy."

Chapter Six

The morning sun shines bright through the window, and the rays leave lines of light down the dark paneling. I throw back the covers and rush to the bathroom, having been woken up by an impatient bladder. I rip open the bathroom door and shriek as Nick struts by me in a towel. Steam trails after him, while drops of water drip down his chest. "What are you doing in my room? You said this was *my* bathroom!"

He pauses in front of me with his toothbrush hanging out the side of his mouth. "It is. It's also the only shower in the house."

Highly annoying. How can I escape thoughts of this man now that I have the scent of him permanently up my nose? "Please get out! I need to use the restroom."

He gives me the up-and-down look, raises his eyebrows, and wiggles them. "Love your…jammies. You're kind of cute when you're angry."

"You weren't supposed to see my short shorts and cami! You're in the guest room!" I reach out to shove him, but I don't want to touch his bare skin, so I end up motioning to him in a shooing manner. "Out! Out! Now!"

"Bossy. I love a woman in charge. I'm going, I'm going."

Between his wet bedhead and the drip of water flirting with his top lip, I barely hear what he's saying.

I rush to the bedroom door and holler after him as I watch him strut down the hallway. "And don't you touch anything in the kitchen. I'm making breakfast!"

"Yes, Ma'am." How this man manages to make every statement sound suggestive, I don't know. The way he looks back at me makes me feel like we just rolled out of the same bed.

I slam the bedroom door. I'm about to pee myself. I make quick work of the shower, wash my long hair as fast as possible and drag a brush through all the curls before doing a quick wet braid down the back. I throw on some deodorant and my favorite cashmere lotion. The ten pounds I intended to lose scream at me as I squeeze into my yoga pants. I hop around the room to get them on. I'm ever so thankful for the oversized lightweight sweatshirt I packed, comfort clothes for the weekend.

I march to the kitchen, determined to repay Nick in some way for his hospitality. Time to show this man I can cook; not that it matters, I tell myself. His collection of vegetables in the fridge is impressive, as is his spice collection in the cupboard. The coffee in the pot brewing smells heavenly. The beeping is perfect timing as I grab a cup. I reach for the coffeepot, eager to get my morning pick-me-up. I freeze as I sense his presence behind me. For a big man, he's awfully good at being silent. His stealth movements must be his army training. I lean to the side as his arm snakes around me to get the coffeepot.

I turn to face him, a movement I regret in seconds, as his face is inches from mine. I feel like an old maid as I clear my throat. "Boundaries."

His eyes set me on fire, and I see nothing but his mouth moving as he answers, "Are meant to be broken."

I lean my head back, as there's nowhere for me to go. "That's not really where I was going with that statement."

He takes a tiny step backward and lifts his coffee cup to

take a sip. “Forgive me, but it’s been a while…since I’ve had a beautiful woman in my home.”

Time for a subject change. I clear my throat and squeak out an answer. “Mushrooms?”

His gaze dances as he continues to stand before me, sipping his coffee. “What?”

“Mushrooms? Do you eat them?!” I’m desperate for any semblance of normal conversation that cannot be misconstrued or lead to the bedroom.

“Easy there, trigger.” He sighs. “Do I have mushrooms in my fridge?”

I wheel around and am so happy to find the fridge so close. I whip it open, thankful for a reason to turn away. “Yes! You have mushrooms.”

“Well then, that would mean I eat them.”

I close the fridge door and turn to him again. “Pans?”

“You know what?” He gives me a wink. “Why don’t I just let you do your thing?”

“Yes.” I clap my hands. “That is an excellent idea. Just go watch your T.V. program or whatever.”

“And miss the chance to watch you prepare my breakfast? Where’s the fun in that? I’ll just hang out here.” He takes a seat at the bar and sets his coffee down.

“Fine.” Great. I have an audience. “This is your home. Sit wherever. Don’t mind me. I’ll just snoop around until I find what I’m looking for.”

He raises his eyebrows at me. “Haven’t you been doing that already?”

Kind of. “Touche’. I guess I deserved that one.”

He taps the countertop. “Oh, hey. The left side of the stove doesn’t work at all, so leave those burners off.”

I flip him a smile. “Good to know.” New idea. Maybe if I irritate him, he’ll leave the kitchen. I turn on John Hiatt and hum along. I’m almost successful in banning Nick from my mind, as I locate my ingredients, crack eggs in the skillet, chop veggies and ham, throw them in there, add just a dusting of cayenne pepper, brown the toast, and sway to the music. I'm quite pleased with the results, as I divvy up two plates. I sit down across from him with my cup of coffee, taking the half-n-half I happily discovered in the fridge, thickening up my coffee with just the right amount. I hold out the half-n-half to him.

"Creamer?"

"Not unless you've got a milk moustache for me to taste." His gravelly voice pings all my nerve endings. All the air has left the room. I think I have hypoxia. I might need a paper bag.

"Excuse me?" I look up, feeling uncertain about his remark and a little scared as I see the intensity of a heat-seeking missile in his eyes.

"I've never seen anyone…sexier than you…in my kitchen…cooking breakfast."

Mind blank. "Did I do something wrong?"

"No." He tosses his fork down on the table, and it lands with a clatter. "That's the problem. You did everything right." He comes out of his chair in a flash and moves jerkily to my side of the table. I stand up because I don't know what's going on.

"Nick."

His hand is on my neck. "I love how you say my name."

"You…you promised to behave."

"I know. And I am, trust me. I'm not doing any of the things that are running through my head right now. If you only knew what I was thinking…"

"Stop." I swallow hard while my jumping pulse against his palm betrays me. I manage to drag my gaze from his face. "I don't want to know. I'm not asking. You need to stop."

"I'm just saying." He moves closer to me, and I can't move a muscle. "I'm just saying you'd give me more credit if you knew the amount of restraint I'm using right now."

"I believe you. What do you want me to—"

His hand guides my gaze back to his, and his thumb gently tilts my chin. I know what's coming, but still the anticipation kills me, as he slowly backs me up against the fridge. There's no escape as his mouth fuses to mine. My hands grip the sides of the fridge, clinging for all I'm worth. If I let go and grab onto him, I'm a goner. As he explores my mouth, his thoroughness melts every bone in my body, leaving me weak in the knees.

Too soon, he releases me, still looking into my eyes, which I'm sure are wide open. My chest heaves as I swallow hard, looking right back at him. "You…You had no right."

He bites his lip for a delicious moment. "I know. I'm sorry. Well, I'm not sorry. I know it's not what you want to hear, but I'm not. Excuse me. I'll be back in about thirty minutes."

I stare past him at his plate. "Your breakfast. It'll get cold."

He looks at me like food is the last thing on his mind. "I can warm it up again. Go ahead and eat. Don't wait on me."

I sit down to eat with shaking hands. I've never felt anything remotely close to what this man makes me feel with just a kiss. I'm in over my head, and nowhere near finding answers for Joy. Dang it. I want to run out the front door and never return. I could always send Daisy up here to question him further. But I can't do that. Joy is my responsibility. I'll just have to ignore the attraction that's getting stronger the longer I know him. Something tells me more complications are coming. I look around the room again, searching for any evidence of a major flaw, which Nick has to have because no sane man can cook like a chef, kiss like that, and not have someone waiting at home for them; unless he's a player. But I didn't see a treasure trove of condoms in his bathroom, unless he keeps them by his bed…*stop thinking about his bed and condoms, Maria!*

I seek sanctuary in the spare room, writing in my diary, trying to clear my head.

Dear Diary,

Forgive me, as I have a conversation with my sister. Well Liz, you'd be ashamed of me. Instead of being brave, I've been a coward. I'm hiding behind a baby girl, of all people. How long can I use her as a shield to guard me from this delicious specimen of a man I've just met? I'm in danger of falling off a cliff. I've already fallen in lust with him, and that feeling could easily change to infatuation, or even love, and I'm terrified. Oh, Liz, I'm in way over my head. I think if you were here, you'd tell me to go for it. We didn't always see eye to eye, but I'd give anything to have you here to argue with.

Diary, I'm back. He has hands I didn't know I dreamed of. I see the strength in them, and it isn't a stretch to imagine them running over my body, feeding the flame that's been there since we first met. When he speaks, my eyes are drawn to his lips, such beautiful instruments of torture, as now I know how they taste. I've never felt a more perfect fit than his lips on mine. His hand on my throat felt nothing like a threat. But none of this matters.

I'm here for Joy, and I need to find answers, but I'm not sure what I'm looking for. He seems like an honorable man. He certainly looks like he could be her father. I can't tell if I'm trying too hard to find a family resemblance, if it's wishful thinking on my part, or if there's something there.

Goal: Find security and stability for Joy.

-Maria

There's a knock at my door. "Yes."

"May I come in?"

I toss my diary behind me on the bed. "How about I come out there?"

He opens the door wide. His gaze shoots right past me. "What have you got there on the bed?"

"That's not your business. It's just something I was reading," I say as I move directly in front of him, standing on tiptoe, as if that's going to block his view.

"What is it?" He looks at my diary for a moment longer before he looks into my eyes. "The best way to get to know someone is their reading material."

"It's nothing." I frown at him, getting more annoyed as his curiosity grows. "Really."

"It's got to be something, since you're so intent on me not seeing it."

"Fine." I throw my hands in the air. "It's my diary. Okay? I keep a diary."

In an unexpected move, he shoves past me, dives on the bed, and snags my innermost thoughts in his outstretched hands, as he lies on his back, holding it out open in front of him, taunting me. I don't even think as I tackle him, struggling in vain to reach my diary, climbing him like a tree. He holds it out of my reach in one hand. His other arm wraps around my waist like a vice grip.

"Maria. Stop moving."

I ignore his warning, still going for my diary. His grip tightens, and he rolls me, pinning me underneath him. The book hits the floor. His elbows rest above my shoulders on the bed, and I'm staring at his Adam's apple, seeing the underside of his freshly shaven chin. My hands move of their own accord to his sides, clutching his tee shirt, but then they sneak under, spanning the broad expanse of his back, trembling as they fan back and forth, lightly scraping. I want to sing as I hear him groan.

"Oh hell. I'm going in."

If I thought I knew what it was to be consumed by desire before, I wasn't even close. His mouth is on my neck, my ear, my face, everywhere but where I want it most. Finally, his breath is mine, and mine is his, as our lips meet, and I am lost, completely immersed in this perfect moment that goes on and on. I can't get enough. I can't feel enough. Apparently neither can he, as the kiss lengthens. I'm burning up. I feel a growing presence pushing up against me. I snap out of it. I turn my head to the side and gasp. He trails kisses on my neck and nibbles on my earlobe. Oh deliciousness. I clear my throat.

"Mercy." The torture continues. "Uncle! I call Uncle!" There's a reprieve.

"What?"

"Stop. Please stop. You're muddling my head. You have to stop."

He rolls off me, lays down beside me, and stares up at the ceiling. "I know this sounds like a line, Maria; but I've never been affected like this, not even close. It's the strongest feeling I've ever felt."

We're both in trouble, and I hate that I can't tell if he's sincere. "I know. Believe me, I know."

He props up on his side and looks down at me. "What are we going to do?"

I turn sideways to look up at him. "What do you mean, what are we going to do? We're adults, Nick. Just practice self-control. You were in the army for twenty years, for goodness sake! Besides, we're not animals. At least I'm not. If you can't control yourself, then keep your distance."

His voice gets all sexy. "You climbed on me."

"You stole my diary! It's private. You're not supposed to read it."

He gives me an ingratiating smile. "How old are you? I thought diaries were for teenagers."

"I'm twenty-two years old." I don't like his tone. "I keep a diary. It's…it's cheaper than therapy." I smack his chest. "Besides, I thought only teenage boys try to read someone else's diary."

"Fine." He clears his throat. "We're equally immature today."

I clear my throat too. "This attraction, while flattering, cannot rule us. So just consider me off limits or whatever."

"For how long?"

"What?"

"How long are you off limits? I mean, if I'm to have a part in Joy's future, and you're to be a part of her future too, then we will be seeing each other quite frequently, I would think."

I can't decide if his persistence is flattering or just plain annoying. "You don't even know if you're her father. I mean, don't you want to take like a paternity test or something?"

"How about I meet her first? I bet I can tell from meeting her if she's family."

This sounds a bit ridiculous, and I can't help but laugh. "You really think you can tell if a six-month-old baby is related to you?"

"It's worth a shot. So, how's about we drive back today, so I can see her?

"Sure." I'll take distance from this man in any form I can get it. "That's a great idea. I'll take my car, and you can take your truck." I hate the way he studies me.

"Nah. I think I'll ride with you. That way we can visit some more on the way to your place."

Five hours in my small car with this man will not be good for my mental health. "How will you return home then?"

He's all nonchalant. "I'll figure it out."

I try again. "What about your work? Don't you have to be back?"

"Thanks for your concern, but I'm on kind of on a sabbatical of sorts? I just retired from twenty years in the army." He looks at me, all amused. "So, I'm not in a rush to look for a source of income."

"Fine, but I'm *not* driving you back, that's all I'm saying."

"No worries. I can take care of myself."

I give him a glare. "So you say, but you're riding with me now?"

He smiles at me as if I were a small child, and I want to slap him.

"What's a better way to get to know the future mother of my child than to take a long car ride?" Ugh. Nick may be hotter than hades, but he's as annoying as a noncompliant patient. He glances at his watch. "Is five minutes long enough for you to pack your things? I'll go gather mine." He jumps up from the bed, and my eyes feast on him as he leaves the room.

Great, just great. There's no escaping him anytime soon. We're going to be in a car together for the next five hours! Why did I agree to such ridiculousness? I hurriedly slam my things into my bag and yank the zipper shut. I think I've got it all as I glance over the empty bed, trying to think straight. I race down the hallway to find him. I don't want to be accused of holding up the show.

Halfway down the hallway, I remember I forgot my diary; but the bed was empty. He got me so flustered he took my diary again.

You've got to be kidding me. I find him in his room, sitting on his bed, reading my diary. Unbelievable. I grab it with one hand, playing tug-of-war, as he holds on to it with an iron grip. I grab it with both hands, but it's no use. His other hand runs up the backside of my leg. My stupid body betrays me, and he knows it, as his eyes stare darkly into mine. I bite down on my lip. He drops my diary. Ha! It's a short won victory, as he yanks me to my knees and pins me between his legs.

"Maria." His husky voice is back. Dang it.

"Nick." I hope I sound as exasperated as I feel.

"Maria, look at me."

I stare harder at the floor. I don't want to, so I don't.

"Maria. Did you mean what you wrote?"

No, I write down my feelings for fun in case some nosy ex-soldier decides to break into my diary. I meet his gaze and glare bullets at him and wait for his head to mentally explode before mine does.

"Well?"

My hands rest on his thighs for balance. I turn my head slightly and stare off to the side and dig in my nails. "Why else would I write it? It's my diary. Those thoughts are personal. They're not meant for you to read."

"But I have, and I can't unread them."

"That's not my fault." My insides quiver. I pinch his legs as hard as I can. He doesn't even wince. "Maybe you should stay out of my diary."

"I can't, Maria. They're your words." He pulls me up against him, and I find resistance is futile as he works his magic with my lips. My fingers dig into his thighs, and I will them to stay where they are. Finally, he pulls away and releases me. "Woman, what are you doing to me?"

I grab my diary and smack his arm with it as I stand to leave. "The feeling's mutual, if that makes you feel any better."

"Then why?" He leans back on his hands. "Then why can't we make good use of this bed? No one will know but us." He's awfully persuasive.

I feel like goody two-shoes, but so what. A girl has her pride. "Because of Joy, and because I have to have self-preservation. And because *I'll* know, and I have to live with myself."

He sighs and holds a hand to his chest. "You're a heart-breaker, Maria."

I laugh and bump his knee with mine. "Come on, big, bad, soldier man. Duty calls."

Chapter Seven

Watching Nick fold his long, tall body into my Honda Fit is almost comical. Almost. As soon as I climb in, the proximity of his big sexy self in my small space makes me feel all claustrophobic. The smell of his body wash and cologne permeates every corner of my car. I feel like he's marking his territory with his smell, even if it's unintentional. I roll down the window just to get some air as we head out of town.

He smiles as he gazes out the window.

"What's on your mind, soldier?"

He turns to me, switches to his bedroom eyes, and runs his finger up and down the inside of my forearm, then the outside of my leg. "Thoughts of this morning. Have no doubt; I've memorized the shape of you; every curve of your body is imprinted in my brain."

"I'm sorry I asked, Mr. Pervy Perv."

"I'm human." He shrugs. "I told you it's been a while."

"What happened with the last one?" I don't know why I'm asking.

His face looks confused. "What makes you think there was a last one?"

I giggle. "Well, your toilet seat was down, which means you're kind of housebroke, so."

"I was engaged once." He frowns. "She got lonely and took up with my best friend while I was deployed. End of story."

"That's terrible, Nick. I'm so sorry. So, your best friend is most likely not the guy who I met at the base and gave me your address."

"What'd he look like?"

"Oh." Time to have some fun. "Very muscular. Sweat-stained workout shirt. Blonde hair, blue eyes. Easy on the eyes, kind of like a model."

"Oh. That'd be Thomas. Let me guess, he hit on you."

"Well, yeah."

"Don't feel special or anything. He hits on anyone female, pretty much."

He just stepped in it.

"And you don't?"

"Guess I'll just have to prove myself." He clears his throat and I feel his gaze on me. "What about you?"

"What about me?"

"Why isn't there any man waiting at home for you?"

"Oh. Well. I kind of took a break from men. I lost someone I loved about a year ago, and it kind of left me empty. I just can't seem to get back to where I was before."

"And was this a man you loved?"

"Um, no." Do I hear jealousy? Surely not. "I lost my…my sister. I've been a little lost ever since."

He reaches over and takes my hand in his. "I'm sorry."

"Thank you. So you know, I've been working full-time, then volunteering quite a bit, filling up my time, so I don't have a lot of down time to think about things, since it doesn't seem to solve anything, and it won't bring her back…so…"

"You're avoiding your grief, then?"

"Maybe. I don't know. I guess I thought if I could help

others, it might ease the pain I feel inside, and I don't do well with nothing to do."

"Did you ever consider therapy?"

Geez, this guy is opinionated as I am! "I'm not suicidal. I'm just sad."

"You don't have to be suicidal to need therapy."

I know that. I'm not stupid. "I've got friends who are sounding boards, and I'd just as soon go to them, thank you very much."

"Alright, just tryin' to help here. Don't get your back up." Says the man who has known me for less than forty-eight hours and is telling me to go to therapy.

I'm still feeling defensive. "I don't *need* your help."

"Apparently. I mean, I'm no expert, but avoidance has never solved any problem that I know of."

Whatever, Nick. I'm facing my problem head on. That's why I came to find you.

"Well, it might solve ours," I say instead. "I'll just keep my distance from you as much as possible."

He chuckles. "Do you really think that's necessary?"

Yes, to keep my sanity and other things intact; definitely yes. This man really pushes my buttons. "Are you serious?! Were you not in your house with me this morning? You practically attacked and mauled me at least once!"

"As I recall, you didn't seem to mind." He smirks, and it grates on my nerves.

"That's not really the point I'm making here. I didn't ask you for any of those kisses, and you darn well know it."

"Fine. But if I wanted to make you beg, you would. Make no mistake about that."

It's a good thing he's so good looking because his arrogance is a huge turn-off. I've got no more answers, so I remain quiet. I'm on simmer, though. I know it's just a matter before I boil over. "So you have sexual prowess, well whoopdee flipping do!"

"What are you, twelve? Besides, you don't know everything. I meant what I said when I've never felt with anyone else what I feel with you! Maybe it's fate or maybe it's just chemistry. Whatever it is, it's off the charts!" His eyes bore a hole in the side of my head.

"Exactly, Nick! It's just chemistry!" I slap the steering wheel. "It doesn't mean anything. You can be attracted to someone who's not necessarily the best person for you." There, that should put him off.

"But What if that person is the right one? Then what?" Nope. He's like a dog with a bone. He won't let up.

"Well, then. I guess that person would have the world by the tail, now wouldn't they? They'd have their soulmate in their sites, and that would be that. All they'd be missing is a white trellis."

He scratches his neck. "You mean like in *Letters to Juliet*?"

"You've seen that movie?" I can't help but smile. "I can't believe you got the reference. It's kind of a chick flick."

"You saying I can't watch it because it's for women?" He nudges me before throwing up his hands. "I'm all for equality, baby."

I snort. "You just objectified me in a thoroughly derogatory manner and totally used that word in the wrong context." Now, I'm smirking.

"Whatever." He rolls his eyes. "I know what I meant. As I was say-ing, it was kind of her favorite movie, and I was just trying to be a good boyfriend. I've seen it so many times I could probably quote it in my sleep."

My heart melts a little. "Well. I guess that's kind of sweet."

"Yep." He sighs. "That's me. I'm just a caring kind of guy." The car goes quiet, but soon, he's clearing his throat. "So. Did I understand you correctly when you said you've never met this baby's mother?"

"Well, yes. I mean, she dropped the baby off after dark on our porch, so we haven't met. But, um, I've had the feeling someone was watching me before this whole thing started."

"You said *our porch*. Who else lives with you?"

So he's a details guy. "Oh. Daisy and Dale."

"What are you, like from the Andy Griffith show? What kind of names are Daisy and Dale?" This man can really stick his foot in his mouth.

"Daisy and Dale are two of my best friends. I've only known them for two months, but they've been a Godsend." I cringe inside at using Daisy's terminology.

"You've only lived in your new place for two months, have brand new friends, and you already trust them implicitly? With my defenseless baby daughter?"

"Stop yelling." This guy is unbelievable. "Are you serious! She may not even be your daughter! And you wouldn't have known about her if it wasn't for me!"

"Okay, okay." He takes a deep breath and massages his temples. "Tell me more about Daisy and Dale."

"They're an old married couple, probably in their seventies at least; hardly capable of being sinister. I live in a house under the new program, where they pair young people to live with the elderly for an equally beneficial outcome for both parties."

"That's a mouthful. So you *chose* to live with an old married couple? Boy, you're just a regular goody-two shoes."

"I am not. I happen to like spending time with them. I…I kind of get annoyed with the majority of people my age. I'm not a ponderous coffee shop girl, and I'm definitely not a barfly. Believe me, I've tried both. Maybe it's my profession that sucks all the fun out of life. I don't know."

"Oh? And what would that be? Are you a librarian?"

And the hits just keep on coming.

"No. But I happen to love libraries. Is there any more room in your mouth, or did you manage to stick your whole foot in yet? Sheesh…I'm a nurse."

"You're a nurse? For real? That's so hot!"

I almost laugh. I swear, why does every guy think that

nurses are hot? If they only witnessed what we do all day, they might change their minds.

"Ugh. I'm not even going to ask why." I laugh to myself. "You could follow me around for a day and watch as I administer enemas and catheters. That'd really get your fire goin'."

"Gross." He makes a face. "Was that imagery really necessary?"

I give him a smirk. "Probably not. I'm just sayin'." There's an uncomfortable silence for a while, and I feel him staring again. "Please stop staring at me. I'm trying to drive."

"Sorry. I'm just trying to figure something out."

I feel him waiting for my reply, but he can just wait. Another big sigh from his side of the car. "So…you thought someone was watching you but did nothing about it?"

"Well. I'm not a soldier, and I'm not in a position to hire a detective, and even though I felt someone's gaze on me, it didn't feel threatening."

"But you never saw anyone who made you curious? Never noticed anyone lingering too long?"

Obviously not, or I would know who Joy's mom is.

"Well. There was this one lady. She had the body of a girl. She was practically skin and bones, not much to her. Her face, though. Her eyes looked like they'd seen too much already. They were hungry and hard. If she's Joy's mother, there was no family resemblance whatsoever."

"Did you talk to her? Sell her anything? If there's a receipt, maybe her name would be on it."

Duh. I would have done that, too, if I had the opportunity. I can't believe how he's questioning my intelligence.

"She didn't buy anything. She kind of danced on the edges at the youth center, looking in, but not getting close enough to make contact."

"Can you remember anything about her that might make her stand out? Tattoos or birthmarks?"

Yes, because I stood around taking pictures of her as she posed.

"No. She was just another homeless lady; hungry, tired, and cold. It may not even be her, but the last time I saw her, she seemed like she wanted to tell me something. I should have tried harder to reach out to her. I could tell she wanted something from me, but I guess I thought she would speak up but now, she's just gone."

"And you're sure this was the mother?"

I glance at him. Does he not hear what I am saying. I don't know. "I'm not sure of anything, Nick, except for Joy's mother doesn't want to be found. Does that description match anyone you might have known about fifteen months ago?"

"Nope. Well, I mean, I don't think so."

"You don't think so? Are the women you sleep with so insignificant to you, you don't remember them?"

He sighs and stares out the window for a while, tapping his fingers against the car door. "A little over a year ago, I lost one of my men. He was young. It was his first deployment. It was a typical test run over ground we'd been on many times before. I practically knew the place like the back of my hand, but that day, something just seemed off. I was extra cautious, and I had given orders; but he didn't follow them. But his loss, I still see his face in my nightmares. I mean, if I'd just gone in ahead of him and checked everything better; or followed my gut instinct that said we needed to get the hell out of there; but that would have been to disobey a direct order from above, and I'm a leader. I couldn't just ignore the order because I had a feeling."

I reach out to take his hand, but he pulls away from me. He has so much pain in his voice.

"So when I came back, I went to visit his family, to try to explain. It's what I would expect. I don't know, somehow I thought if I could just meet with them and give them answers, but none of that helped. They were so kind and understanding about the whole thing, and that was so much worse than if they had yelled at me or asked me to leave. After that, I was all tore up inside, and I kind of went on a month-long bender. There were some nights I got so drunk I didn't know if I would wake up the next morning, but I couldn't seem to stop. I kept thinking I could drink away the pain and the disappointment in myself for losing him. I kept thinking if I drank enough, I could stop the nightmares."

I squeeze his hand. "It wasn't your fault. He didn't follow orders."

"I know. But it doesn't help the fact that he's gone. We give orders as a precaution, but orders can't prevent catastrophe, and knowing all this doesn't make losing someone any easier. So if I ran into this girl during that time, anything could have happened. It's hard to say. And, I know how it sounds, but it's the truth."

I don't know what to think, except this man might be too honest for his own good. "It'd be easier to be mad at you if you'd give me excuses."

He laughs and his whole face lights up. "So now you're asking me to lie to you? That's a first."

"That's not what I said." I smack his arm.

"Well, I'm tired. I think I'll get some shut eye since you're driving."

Thank goodness. I'm about done with all his questions.

He turns away from me and lays the seat down. I see skin as he drags his hoodie over his head and wads it up in a ball. "Stop starin' at my ass," he growls out.

I can't help but giggle as I keep my eyes on the road. I reach out to turn up the radio and jam out to Pink. Pretty soon I'm singing along, "Please, please don't leave me…"

There's a faint groan from Nick. "Oh Lord, help me, she can sing like an angel," he mutters as he covers his ear with his hand. The rest of the drive goes surprisingly fast. About an hour from home, we're driving through a small town, all peaceful and quiet. I can't help but smile at all the Christmas decorations in the business windows. Nick reaches over and grabs my wrist. He startles me so I almost drive off the road. He's sleeping with shades on so dark, I can't see his eyes, and he hasn't moved a muscle for the past few hours.

"Hey. Let's stop at the bakery."

"Alright." We head inside and the aroma draws me to the glass display case.

I watch as he walks along, one hand on his chin, his eyes all alight, making me giggle.

"What? What's so funny?"

"You are! You should see your face. You look like a little boy in front of a birthday cake."

"I enjoy food. What's wrong with that?" He pouts a little.

I shouldn't find a grown man acting childish so cute. "Nothing." I roam over the baked goods behind the glass.

"What are you going to have?" His dark gaze caresses me.

"Oh, probably anything with chocolate. That chocolate croissant looks good. I love dark chocolate, because it's warm, sweet, and melty, with just the right amount of bitterness."

He leans in, breathing on my ear as he talks. "You sure you're only talking about chocolate?"

I punch his arm and he backs off with a laugh.

"Gotcha. I think I'll have that sweetbread roll with a touch of cayenne. I like it curvy and stacked, with a touch of sass." He winks at me and raises an eyebrow.

I put my hands on my hips and make a face. "That doesn't even deserve a response."

He gets all sweet-faced and sincere. "Would you like to go for a walk? I saw a bridge a ways back. I'd like to stretch out before getting back into your tin can you call a car."

I ignore the dig he made about my car as I look up at him, batting my eyelashes. "Nick, are you asking me on a date?"

I get an eye roll in response. "I might consider it, but you said you weren't interested. C'mon. Let's walk."

We walk through town, and I have fun checking out all the little mom-and-pop stores with their window decorations. The town park has a little lake, and we walk the path around it. We stop to stand in the middle of the covered bridge, staring out at the water. Nick leans over the edge, and drops breadcrumbs down below, chuckling as the ducks and the fish fight over them.

An elderly couple walks by and Nick turns to me and winks. He pulls out his phone and draws me toward him. I play along, lean back on his chest, and look up to take a picture. I can't help but notice that we fit perfect together, as my head stops just below his chin.

The elderly lady approaches in her bright purple pants, tangerine sneaks, and neon-green hoodie. She's stylin'. She smiles up at Nick. "Would you like me to take your picture?"

"Yes, ma'am. That'd be wonderful." He shoots her a mega-watt grin, making the old lady blush. I cross my arms across my waist as I lean back into him again. I pinch his side hard as I grin at the camera. He wraps one long arm around my waist while the other sneaks behind me and taps my butt. It takes all I've got not to react as the little lady takes another picture. I quick step away from him and hold out my hand for his phone. His other hand grabs mine, and I can't help noticing that it feels so right.

He pulls me toward him, and I'm a fish on a line. I'm hooked on Nick Laus. What am I going to do? My confusion must show on my face, as he frowns down at me.

"You got a stomachache? You look constipated."

"Wow. I can honestly say I've never been told that before." I drop his hand and walk faster.

"You sure are prickly."

Wouldn't you be if I told you were constipated?

I stop and spin around to face him. My voice raises while my hands fly about wildly. "I'm not prickly. I don't like being toyed with. And I don't like being the object of your affection whenever you get the urge. You need...you need to keep your hands and lips to yourself!"

"Fine. I'll try harder. But if you only knew how good you taste...and how good you look in your little yoga pants and cotton sweatshirt. Your cooking styles gets my fire going, and that little mole above your lip, well, it does something to me. And I love how your long black hair flows down your back, leading to your curvy backside—

have mercy."

"Alright! I get it! Stop. Just...please be quiet."

"I just wanted to be sure you know I'm attracted to you."

"Yeah. I think I figured that one out. Let's just stop thinking about all that. We need to focus on baby Joy."

"What are you going to do if she's not mine? Are you...are you going to take her to foster care?"

"No." I shake my head back and forth. "No, I can't. I would never do that." My last sentiment comes out more like a whisper. I'm staring at the ground. I look back at Nick. I'm all flustered. "I don't know what I'll do, but foster care is not a choice. I mean, I suppose I'll enroll in foster care classes, as long as they let me keep her, and then adoption would be the next step."

"Adoption! Maria, you just met her. You're just going to go from being single to being a mother? Isn't that a bit rash?" He has a point, and ordinarily that's the advice I would give anyone else, but now that I've met Joy, I can't let her go.

"Her circumstances are not her fault, Nick. I don't think anyone's going to come looking for her. I can't take her back. I won't. She deserves everything I can do for her. She's an innocent baby who needs a home."

"This is crazy." He stares me down. "Have you thought all of this through? I mean, this is a lifetime you're talking about."

I sit down on the nearby bench to gather my thoughts before I look up at him. "Nick, I know that, but sometimes you don't choose your life, it chooses you. I feel like I've been given a chance to do something great, something for someone else. I can't walk away from her. I just…I'd never forgive myself."

He sits down and twirls the end of my braid with his finger. "I can't wait to meet her."

"We need to get to the car." I pull away from his hand. "We've still got a drive. It's time to get back on the road."

He reaches out his hand to help me up, but I stand up on my own. His hand remains open. "What?"

"Give me the keys. I'm driving."

It's very tempting. "It's my car, Nick. I don't think so. No one drives Chloe but me."

"Chloe?" He makes a face. "You named your car, Chloe?"

"Yeah, so what." I nod. "I'm a Drew Barrymore fan."

He's more confused. "So why didn't you name your car Drew?"

I sigh. "Chloe was a chihuahua in *Beverly Hills Chihuahua*, and I loved her character, so that is the name of my car."

Another eye roll. "You really get into your movies." He looks at me for a response. I give him none. He holds out his hand again. "Please, may I drive the most beautiful, oversized lawnmower, *named Chloe,* that I've ever seen?"

I can't help but giggle. "Make fun all you want. She gets great gas mileage, and she's never let me down yet."

"Alright, already. Can I drive her then?"

"Only because I'm tired, and as long as you acknowledge that I've never let anyone else drive her." He follows me down the short path to the lot.

"Gee. You really know how to make a guy feel special."

I hand off the keys. Nick misses no opportunity. He grabs my hand briefly, skims his fingers, feather light, along my wrist and into my palm, giving me the shivers. We walk across the lot. I try to lose my goosebumps as we climb into Chloe. I feel out of place as I climb into the passenger side. I take in Nick as he sits behind my wheel. My seating position isn't the reason I have butterflies.

After a great amount of theatrics from Nick, moving the seat as far back as it will go, clearly demonstrating his arm easily spans the length of my car as he leans toward the middle with his arms outstretched, he decides Chloe's drivable. Sounds of classic country bounce off my windowpanes. I turn away from him and curl up in the laid down seat, unsuccessfully ignoring that I'm loving the scent of him on his wadded-up hoodie I use as a pillow. He grabs my foot, drags it over his knee, and removes my shoe, smooth as butter, one-handed. He rubs my socked foot as he's driving. I want to take it back, but his thumb feels so nice on my heel. He's really got a thing for physical touch, but this time I'm not complaining.

I wake to the GPS voice, "You have reached your destination" repeating itself. I move my foot from his knee, embarrassed.

He waves my shoe back and forth. "I think you lost something."

I look into his eyes. I feel his touch through every part of me and I can't shake it. I've lost more than just my shoe. I'm strangled by the air, or the lack of it.

"I lost nothing. You took my shoe." I snatch it back, grumpily, and yank it back on. I hop out of the car and walk up the drive. I'm anxious to see Joy.

Chapter Eight

The front porch door flies open, and Daisy stands in front of me, holding Joy out like a trophy. "Maria! You're home! And you brought a visitor." She hands Joy to me like an afterthought, in her hurry to get to Nick.

"Hi! I'm Daisy! Welcome to my home. Oh, it's so nice to meet you in person. We've read all about you! Oh, phooey. That came out all wrong. Where are my manners?! Please. Come inside." She grabs Nick's hand, and with more strength than I thought she possessed, starts dragging him up our front porch steps. It's quite a sight; tiny, gray-haired Daisy hauling Nick, the big, tall, imposing soldier, into her home.

He follows along like a puppy, but not before he turns and raises one eyebrow at me as he goes. Joy and I follow close behind.

The meeting of the men is a strange sight. Dale stands up from the kitchen table chair, sticks out his chest, and rocks back on his heels. He then stands on his tiptoes and does his best to look down his nose at Nick. None of this works, of course, because while Dale is a good-sized man, he's still an inch or two shorter than Nick. Nick gives him a kind smile in return, which seems to only make things worse as Dale approaches. "I'm Dale. Just think of me as Maria's guardian."

Color me embarrassed.

"Don't you mean Joy's guardian, Dale?" I say out of desperation, trying to lighten the mood.

"I meant what I said. I consider myself your guardian, as well as Joy's. So tell me, young man, what are your intentions here?"

Nick clears his throat. "My intentions, sir, are as unclear to me as they are to you. I only heard about Joy yesterday. As far as Maria, my intentions don't really matter. It's whatever she decides. I'm sure you've noticed Maria has a mind of her own."

"Maria deserves only happiness and love," Dale answers boldly. "She's already been hurt enough."

Dale's boldness makes me want to fall through the floor. Things just got more awkward, and I didn't think that was possible.

Daisy claps her hands loudly between them. "If you two are going to squabble over a grown woman who can make her own choices, the girls and I are going to leave. This is nonsense! Now, Nick. Would you like to officially meet Joy?" She doesn't wait for an answer, as she takes Joy from my arms and transfers her to Nick.

I don't know what I expected to happen, but I feel betrayed in every sense of the word as Joy's chubby little fingers reach up to touch Nick's chin. She runs her fingers along his five o'clock shadow. Nick gives her the biggest grin I've seen on him yet, and her little smile soon turns to a gurgling baby giggle, followed by a huge smile. My heart melts, and I find I can't stay jealous of his winning her over so easily.

They look at each other for a while, and Nick takes on a more serious expression. Joy stares into his eyes. He studies her with a quiet intensity, holding his poker face steady. As she waits for his expression to change, her little chin starts to quiver, and I react. I have no idea what he's thinking, and it's driving me crazy. I can't take the scrutiny Joy must feel, or the fact that she's about to start bawling.

I swoop in and take her in my arms, trying my best to loosen her from his gentle hold. This only succeeds in my front bumping up against him, pressing into his arms and fingers as my back rests against his chest. He doesn't let go of her until he's cradling me along the length of him. I didn't want this proximity, but it's the only way I feel safe holding—who am I kidding—stealing Joy back, as I can't stand the thought of Nick looking at this innocent baby girl like she's got a motive. Her little face relaxes when I smile at her. I hold her against me and let her angel chin rest on my shoulder. Her little legs move up and down against my chest. Her tiny hands reached out to Nick, who I catch in the wall mirror making faces at my sweet Joy, as he sneakily caresses my shoulders, torturing me with his touch. Nick holds us both captive. An escape route occurs to me.

"I think she's wet. I'll just go and change her." I break away from his embrace as I feel his thumb brush the base of my neck.

He follows close behind me, as if he's suddenly afraid to leave me alone with her. I stand there, holding Joy like a shield, as I look accusingly at Nick, waiting for him to leave the room. "Well? Aren't you going to change her? I thought you said she was wet."

"Are you going to leave so I can?"

"I need to know how to change a diaper. It'd be better if I could learn by watching you, don't you think? Besides, if she sees you trust me, then maybe she won't be scared when I change her."

"Fine." Sheesh. There's no getting rid of this guy. He's stuck to my side like glue. "I suppose you have a point." I barely remove her diaper when Nick snatches her up. He turns her around and stares at her behind!

"Hey! What in the heck are you doing?"

He looks bewildered at first, but a slow smug grin takes the place of his discerning frown. He nods his head up and down excitedly. "She's definitely mine. That's my birthmark." He motions with his head in a forward manner, as he holds her backside level with his face.

All I see is Joy slipping from his fingers, going straight to the floor. "Easy! Don't hold her out like that. What if you drop her?"

"Look closely." He ignores my warning cries. "She's got a small brown birthmark in the dimple of her right lower back just above her butt cheek that looks kind of like a comma. I've got one just like it. If you don't believe me, I'd be happy to show you," he says as he hands her over. He starts to unbutton his jeans.

"Hey! Stop right there. Keep your pants on. I don't need to see any of that."

"Relax. Aren't you a nurse? Surely you've seen people's butts before? Besides, it's not just that she has a butt birthmark, it's the right shape and color too!"

"Don't worry." I turn away from him, happy to be distracted by cleaning Joy and sprinkling her with a little baby powder. I let her lay here a few minutes to air out as she kicks her legs with glee. "I believe you. But that doesn't necessarily mean you're related. I mean, lots of people have unexplainable, strange birthmarks."

"What are the odds?" I hear his zipper close. He walks over. "You want to google the statistics on the average number of unrelated people who have matching butt birthmarks, go right ahead. I think it's a sign. Besides, look at the color of her hair and her eyes. She's definitely got my eyes."

I don't want to see Nick's eyes every time I look at Joy's. I love her wide-eyed innocence.

"She may have your eyes, but she doesn't have the lusty pervy perv factor."

"Aw yes." He laughs! "Poor girl doesn't know how to appreciate a figure like an hourglass, lips as soft and full as rose petals, hair that looks like satin…"

I wheel around. "Shut up, Nick. Please. Don't you get tired of rattling off that nonsense?"

His eyes narrow at me. "Who made you so cynical? It's not nonsense. It's the truth. Besides, just give her time, she'll learn to appreciate the opposite sex."

"Don't be so superficial! Someone's looks do not encapsulate who they are! Plus, what you said is a gross mis-exaggeration of my physical attributes." I stare him down.

"Don't try and tell me what I see!" He frowns down at me. "I think I can figure that out for myself." He returns my stare with one of his own. I'm getting hotter and hotter. He gives me hyperthermia.

Time to change the subject. "So you're saying you think she's yours, and you don't want to take a DNA test? What are your plans for her in the future?" I ask as I quickly wrestle Joy into a diaper.

"Right now I'd love to lay her down on her playmat by the fireplace and watch her do her thing." Having said that, he waltzes over, leans over Joy, tickles her tummy, and hip bumps me before swooping her into his arms. He turns to me, pecks me on the lips, and takes her back to the other room, and lays her down. He sits beside her on the mat on the floor.

I go and sit across from him. He reaches out after my hand, but I dodge him. He looks at me for an answer because I know it's going to get to him. "I'm not holding your hand in front of her, not when we don't know anything about what's happening next. It feels dishonest." I sound like a prude, but I don't care. My life is already complicated enough with Joy. I don't need to add a red-hot love affair to it.

"Maria. She's a baby! She won't remember much of anything she sees."

"That's not the point. I want an open, honest relationship with her, and it won't be if I lie to her from the beginning.

Like you said, her future is a big decision, not to be taken lightly. I've got to be certain of who will be here for her." I get a glare in return.

"I'm the only one who might possibly have a legal tie to Joy by law. You'd do well to remember that." He speaks soft and low, but his words hit me like a ton of bricks.

"Trust me, I remember." Desperation fills me and I grasp at straws. "Are you seriously going to blackmail me into holding your hand?" I stare back at him, but he says nothing. His jaw clenches. "Besides, I have a letter. That means something."

"Not really, Maria." He crosses his arms on his chest. "Anyone could have written that letter. There's no way to prove otherwise. You could possibly be charged with kidnapping."

"This is ridiculous." I glare back at him. "You wouldn't know she exists if not for me. Her *mother* gave Joy to me. I am *not* a kidnapper! Daisy and Dale are my witnesses! They found her on the porch." I glare at him. He's infuriating!

"I would never accuse you in a court of law. I'm merely pointing out that by law, at this moment, you have no legal rights to her." His eyes soften slightly as he sits a while longer, watching her. His expression grows more strained. He jumps up. "I need some air. I'm taking a walk."

I watch Nick go. Isn't it just like a man to walk off and leave me with the baby when times get hard? What am I thinking? I wanted him to go. I should be happy. My head hurts, but not as much as the pain in my heart. I smile at Joy, but I'm coming apart inside. How is any of this going to work? I can't give her up. We need each other.

Chapter Nine

Me and my big mouth. I was afraid. I spoke out of fear and anger. I reach out to Joy. I love how she smiles so big at me and wraps her little hand around my finger. Her feet kick happily. She turns over and gets up on her hands and knees! She starts rocking back and forth. I think she's going to crawl! I feel awful, but I lay her on her back before I jump up and run to find Nick. I holler his name. "Nick! Nick!" The house door slams. He sprints past me.

I run after him. I stop as I see his whole body tensed, standing in one spot, staring down at Joy, as if he's poised to spring into action. He turns towards me. "Why'd you yell at me like that? I thought she was hurt. I thought something awful happened."

"I'm sorry. I thought…I thought she was getting ready to crawl, and I didn't want you to miss it." I wring my hands in worry.

All seriousness leaves his face as he drops down to the floor. He gets down on his knees and elbows, and rests a small distance from Joy, who's back to rocking on her hands and knees. His hands reach out. "Come on, baby girl, crawl over here. You know you want to."

Joy's dark eyes sparkle as she gurgles. Slowly she reaches out one hand towards him, tips onto her chin, and bumps the floor. I rush to pick her up. Nick's voice stops me. "Don't. She won't learn if you don't let her fall."

"Nick. She's just a baby."

"Is she crying? Is she bleeding?"

I look at little Joy. She grunts as she puts her little fist into the carpet, already pushing herself up again. Her stubborn determination casts a strong suspicion that she must be Nick's daughter. Soon, she's up on all fours again. Her dark head of curls hangs down like a charging bull. I watch with eager anticipation as she raises her fist once more, then puts it back down, making a slight movement forward. She soon follows with the other hand. The look of triumph on her face over this small discovery is priceless. I know it won't be long and she'll be motoring all over the house.

Nick turns to look at me. The pride in his face is unmistakable. I'm in deep trouble of falling so hard and so fast. A seed of doubt pops into my head, which I hate, but it's there. Would Nick be interested in me if Joy weren't part of this complicated equation? What if he takes Joy and meets someone else? He's charming, funny, smart, and sexy. He could have any woman he wants, so why would he want me? I'm rather ordinary compared to him.

I turn away from him, as it hurts too much to see all the hope there. I look over at Daisy and Dale standing in the doorway. They too are mesmerized by Joy's new milestone, as Daisy locks eyes with me, giving a little clap of her hands, then raising her fists up in victory.

Dale chuckles, never tearing his eyes from Joy. "That's my girl."

I wipe a tear of pride away and glance at Nick. Joy is our girl. But for how long?

Chapter Ten

The best thing about Nick staying over is with him sleeping in the guest bedroom, Joy is back in my room. Her little body is a natural heater as she sleeps snuggled up to my side. I try to stay awake and watch her blissful, peaceful sleep and smell her sweet baby breath as little puffs of air blow across my cheek. There's nothing sweeter or more angelic than a sleeping baby, particularly little Joy. All of a sudden, the day catches up with me, and my eyes won't stay open.

I wake with a start in the morning, once more to an empty bed. I jump up to go to the kitchen and remember I stripped down to a skimpy tee and my underwear, as I got too hot in the night. I throw on a pair of sweats and a hoodie. The cold tile on the kitchen floor gives me a start. I hear Nick's low voice and Joy's sweet gurgle. I turn around and head back to my bed, thankful for one more day off. I burrow into the covers, but it's no use. Twenty minutes later, I'm still awake. Darn it.

Dear Diary,

I'm not sure what to write, and this has never happened before. Nick is a wonderful guy, way out of my league (in looks anyways). I don't know what to think about our future together, whether or not we have one, apart from Joy.

Joy had a huge milestone yesterday! She crawled for the first time and that was pretty amazing! We were all so proud of her. It was a beautiful moment!

Nick makes me nervous. I can't always tell what he's thinking. I don't regret looking him up, but I don't want to lose Joy. I must do what's best for her, even if it kills me.

Goal: Be less defensive with Nick.

-Maria

I smell coffee and pancakes. Daisy must be up. I head back to the kitchen again. Daisy has crumbled a pancake to pieces on a plate and Joy is messing in it to her little heart's content. There's pancake crumbs everywhere; on the floor, in her hair, in her fingers. I can't help but notice only a very small percentage makes it to her mouth. We all sit around the table, enthralled by Joy and her bubbly antics over a pancake. I sit down with my cup of coffee. Nick peeks over at my cup, gets up and brings back the milk, lightening my coffee. I tap my finger impatiently on the table. Something's up. I can feel it.

Daisy eyeballs my tapping finger. I eyeball her back and continue; my foot joining in the tapping. Daisy takes a deep breath and I know I'm going to be annoyed by what she says next. "Maria. You know how I was talking to you about finding another renter? Well, Nick has graciously accepted my offer. He's going to live here until we get this whole Joy situation figured out. It couldn't be better timing. He told me how he just retired from the army, and he's not tied to any job right now, so he can basically move anywhere. And he's a handyman! So, how great is that?"

My finger taps faster. Nick reaches over and lays a hand over mine. "Relax, Maria."

I jump up, almost spilling my coffee, whisper-shouting at Nick. "Don't tell me to relax! We've got to talk." I head back to my room, walking past Daisy. "Excuse us for a minute, Daisy."

She turns to smile at Nick. "Take your time." Daisy's tone is full of suggestion. She's such a scheming brat.

Nick gets up from the table, looking all innocent as he follows me out of the room, while I tear down the stairs, listening for him to make sure he doesn't head off in another direction. I can't believe he went behind my back and talked Daisy into letting him stay. As soon as he's in my room, I reach behind him and close the door. "Just what do you think you're doing? I never said you could stay here."

"Well. Technically, it's a three-person vote, and Daisy and Dale agreed, so your vote doesn't matter." His smug smile is more than I can take. I see red.

"So this whole thing was your idea? You talked two innocent elderly people into feeling sorry for you, and you're staying here now. Living in *my* house?"

His eyes sparkle back at me. "You're so hot when you're mad."

I stomp my foot and try to ignore the fact that I'm acting like a toddler. "Shut it down, Nick, and focus."

He grins even more and holds up a finger. "First of all, this house is equally shared by the three of you, so only a third of it is yours. But, if you're going to have a conniption, I'll find a rental. Either way, I'm sticking around. I need to be close by in case Joy needs anything. You know, since I'm her father and all."

"You still don't have proof you're her father!" I'm so mad I poke his chest. "Who do you think you are, moving into my house without my permission? You wouldn't even know about

Joy if I hadn't looked you up. We were doing just fine without you."

"Were you?" His face fills with disbelief. "You had her all of not even a whole day, and you immediately came looking for me. Why did you do that if you say you were doing just fine?"

"It was Daisy's suggestion." I poke his chest again. "She practically shoved me out the door to find you! And I had four days off, so the timing was good." I hope I sound more sure than I feel.

He steps into my space and smirks down at me.

"What?"

"It sounds an awful lot like fate to me. It seems the only person fighting our attraction is you." His hands on my arms mess with my concentration, and I knock them away.

"Stop touching me!"

He takes a step back and holds his hands in the air. "Have you even tried to take her to the doctor since you've had her? What do you think will happen? I've got a pretty good idea. They would wonder how a woman with no legal papers and is not the mother has custody of her. That's what would happen. Did the absent mother provide you with Joy's shot record? Did you come looking for me in order to get the rest of the information on Joy?" His questions hang in the air, and I can't answer any of them.

"Nick." I hate that he's causing me to doubt my own intentions. "I came looking for you because I thought it was the right thing to do. No, I hadn't even thought as far as medical appointments and shot records, but I'm sure she's up to date on everything. Her mother might have been a little messed up, but I think she had good intentions with her daughter, just like I do. I'm trying to do the right thing by Joy, and that's why I contacted you." Arguing with Nick is exhausting. He's way too good at a much-needed reality check.

"Well, what would happen if there was an emergency?

What would happen if you tried to ask for a shot record? Do you think they would give it to you; a person who is not her mother or her legal guardian? I'm just saying you're not exactly prepared."

"You're right." I sigh. "I'm not prepared for every situation, but soon I will be. I've got plans. And technically, she's only been with me for *two* days."

"Okay, fine. But at least acknowledge the fact that in all of these scenarios, I'm the easiest solution. Me. I'm her father. They would give all of that information to me. No questions asked. I only want to help Joy. I only want to take care of her." He steps closer to me, rubs his hands up and down my arms, and brushes the base of my neck with his thumb. "And you too, if you'd just let me."

"That's what I'm talking about." I shove him away. "You can't *do* that if you're staying here. No hanky panky. Our focus should be on Joy. That's it." I step towards the door.

"I'll back off if you really want me to, but I don't think you do." He's frowning again. "Your mouth says no, but the rest of you says something else."

Then quit looking at my mouth.

"Oh, get over yourself. Just ignore the attraction. I am… anyway, who came in and got Joy this morning?"

His face goes blank. "What do you mean?"

"You know what I mean. She was in my bed last night and then this morning I woke, and she wasn't here." I stare at him.

His smirk is back. "Why is that important?"

I cough. "It was you. You came in here when I wasn't completely dressed…and you…"

"And I got Joy. End of story."

My cheeks are burning. This is so dumb. He came into my room and invaded my privacy. He should be the one embarrassed, not me. "Why did you come and get her? Was she crying? I didn't hear anything."

"Your little matchmaker, Daisy, told me to come and get

her. She told me Joy was probably hungry. So I came and got her. What's the big deal? I mean, would you rather Dale come in and see you half naked?"

No. Definitely not.

"I just told you. I don't like the idea of you coming in my room, seeing me when I'm not fully dressed or awake. It's an invasion of privacy. You may not care who sees you and your junk, but I do. This is my body."

"Yes. And what a fine one it is. Next time, I'll knock. And wake up the whole house. To preserve your dignity. Are you done scolding me? I'd really like to go finish my coffee while it's still lukewarm. I'll start looking for a place to rent." He heads for the door.

Now I feel like a raging witch. "No, Nick. It's okay. You can stay here. You're right. You do have more rights to Joy than anyone else. And I'm sure I can handle you living here, as long as you respect the boundaries. I've got to have boundaries."

Nick whips around, smiling his mega-watt, turn-my-insides-to-mush smile, stepping so close to me, his nose almost touches mine, as he hovers. "Boundaries, huh? You keep telling yourself, that, sweetheart; but here's the thing. I've never been able to stay inside the lines." His hot breath touches my lips with every word. He stays as still as a tree for what seems like forever. His breath warms my lip, and I'm waiting, and then I'm wanting, so bad, but I'm not fulfilled. Just when I think he's going to stay here all day, camped out less than a fraction of a hair from my lips, the sexual tension building steadily between us, he steps backward, never breaking eye contact.

"Boundaries," he whispers. He's such a tease. He struts past me out the door, leaving my insides quaking. What am I going to do with Nick Laus, who's far from being a saint.

Chapter Eleven

I barely sit down on the bed to catch my breath from Nick's latest assault on my senses and there's a knock!

I throw open the door. He's back. He looks all hot and cozy in a dark green sweater and a pair of jeans that fit just right. He cradles precious Joy in his arm. "Come on, Maria, we've got places to go." He looks me up and down. "Throw on a light-colored sweater. It'll look nicer."

"Why?"

He ignores me and raises his eyebrow. "Maybe make it a little snug, so I can see all your curves." He gives me a saucy wink as he walks away, whistling while Joy's chubby fingers pat his face. How I envy her fingers.

I turn away, muttering to myself. "Maria. Snap out of it."

"We're leaving in five minutes, with or without you," he calls from the other room.

Where is he taking Joy without me?

I'm not ready to let him take Joy anywhere without me, and he knows it. Drat. I dig through my sweaters and find a light-colored one. I yank it over my head, grab the lip gloss off my dresser and a hairbrush, and clip. I run out the door to

Nick's rumbling truck. I blink. "How did that get here so fast?"

He winks at me. "Don't you worry about it. I have my own connections." I'm happy to see Joy looking all safe and sound in her car seat. I haul my leg up and climb up in the front seat.

Nick shoots me an innocent grin like we haven't been fighting all morning. "I'm so glad you're coming. I have no idea what dress to buy her. She needs some new clothes. I'm tired of the clothes she came in. Where do we go for baby clothes?"

I glance at her. I feel so bad. Why didn't I think of these things? "I guess we could go to the mall. They have a few baby stores there."

His eyes twinkle. I think I just got played. "Sounds perfect. The mall it is." He drives with utmost care, and it takes us twice as long to get there, but I say nothing. I feel cherished and safe. Nick attaches a drawstring nylon bag on his back.

"What's in the bag?"

"Oh. That's my diaper bag." He cringes at the word.

"You put diapers in there?" I bite back a smile.

He looks at me like it's obvious. "Well, I'm not carrying a woman's bag around, I know that. So I just emptied my gym bag and threw some stuff in." His look of discomfort is quite enjoyable.

"Stuff?"

"Yeah. Baby-changing stuff. Are you done with the inquisition?"

I help Joy out of her seat and hand her down to Nick from up in the truck. I climb down and take her back. I hold Joy on my hip. "Yeah. We're ready."

As soon as we step in the mall, I remember why I haven't been to the mall this winter. There's Christmas lights, Christmas music, and a giant Christmas tree. The place is plumb full of holiday spirit, and I'm feeling none of it. Christmas was my sister's favorite holiday, and it's so hard to be here without her. I scan the mall directory and find the store. "There it is. It might be a little walk."

"Let's walk slow." Nick smiles at Joy. "I love to watch her eyes light up at everything. It's so cool to imagine her seeing everything for the first time. Tell me if you get tired, and I'll take a turn carrying her."

We walk by the escalator, and I see the rent-a-strollers that look like animals. "Oh, Nick. I bet she'd love one of those." We pick out a giraffe, and Nick sticks his card in to release the stroller. He takes Joy from me and sets her in the seat. Her hands tap excitedly on the handle and she smiles from ear to ear. She gurgles and coos as she points to the lights in the store windows. We get to the store and Nick cracks me up as he starts tossing outfits left and right into the shopping bag. "Nick. Slow down. She doesn't need all this."

He gives me a look. "I'm making up for lost time. Besides, she'll look so cute in these."

I expect Nick to wait outside, but he walks in the dressing room, and together we wrestle Joy into a few outfits to be sure we have the right size. Joy tolerates it for a little while, but by the third outfit, she starts fussing. We take a break. I reach into his bag and find the container of dry cereal. Nick brings out a bright red dress with layers and layers of chiffon. Joy's eyes light up. She claps her hands and holds them out. I can't help but laugh.

"It looks like Daddy knows his girl." I swallow hard as the words slip out before I can stop them.

Nick freezes for a half second. The air feels heavy. He coughs a little. "Help me get this on her."

Joy's as cute as a Christmas angel in her shiny new dress. She looks up at us, as if waiting for our approval. I ooh and ah over her. Nick picks her up and holds her in front of the mirror. Joy smiles at her own reflection. He sets her down carefully in the stroller and hands the cereal to me. "Here. I'm going to pay for all these clothes."

I push the stroller off to the side and watch Joy as she munches happily on her cereal. I can't help but notice the women walking by Nick. Many of them give him a second look. He doesn't seem to care. He only has eyes for Joy. He shoves the bags into the bottom of the stroller, takes my hand and we walk out of the store. We go along, and it feels so strange, but so right. With Nick, I feel grounded. I feel secure. There's a permanence about him. I know he's a man who will stay when the going gets tough. All of a sudden, I'm drowning in emotion, and I don't know how to stop it.

"Maria?" Nick's voice pulls me from my reverie. "Are you alright?"

I clear my throat. "Of course, Nick. Why wouldn't I be?" I look up. We're standing in the Santa line. "Nick, what are we doing?"

"It's Joy's first Christmas, Maria. She's going to see Santa."

"Why don't you and Joy take the picture?" This feels too much like a fake family picture. "I'll just stand off to the side and take your picture. I don't like my picture taken."

"I want you in the picture with us, Maria." Nick answers soft and low. "You make Joy happy."

I teeter on uncertainty. This is all so new. I study Nick holding Joy. Their dark eyes sparkle and twinkle. They're the perfect pair. I feel all alone. Even though it's my own fault, I'm not brave enough to let Nick all the way in. What if he doesn't stay? I don't know how much more loss I can take. I never should have looked him up. Plowing through piles of red tape to adopt Joy would be easier on my heart than Nick and his devastating effect on my senses.

He clears his throat. He looks directly at me. "You make *me* happy."

My stomach bottoms out, and I swear my knees buckle. I paste on a smile as Joy stares down at me. "I'm doing this for Joy."

He gives my hand a squeeze. "I'll take it."

Soon it's our turn, and Joy's so brave. She doesn't even cry when she sits on Santa's lap. She's too busy pulling on his long white beard. The camera flashes, and it's like she was born to it, as she gives a little laugh, and then a big cheesy grin. There's another flash. Santa hands her back. "You all have a Merry Christmas! Ho! Ho! Ho!"

Nick sets Joy back in the stroller. We stroll through the mall one more time before we park it. I carry the shopping bags. Nick carries Joy.

We get back to the house, and Joy's tuckered out. She's sound asleep in her car seat. I barely get in the house, and Daisy meets me in the kitchen. She hands me a big mixing bowl. "Here, I started this, but I'm too tired. You and Nick can finish it."

I should fight Daisy's meddling ways, but suddenly, I'm in the mood for baking. I take the chilled bowl and toss a little flour on the counter. I start rolling. I go for the cookie cutters. Nick shows up beside me.

"Let me help."

I don't need your kind of help, Nick. You're so hands-on I can't think straight.

"Oh, you don't have to." I try to sound all nonchalant.

"I know. I want to."

Take a hint, already. Go away.

"Okay." I'm determined to sound uninterested, even though I'm kind of interested. I think.

He peels off his sweater. He's wearing a soft cotton tee underneath, the kind that fits him way too well. I see a hint of skin above his jeans before he tugs it back down. He gives me an ornery grin. "What you lookin' at?"

I blink. I look at the stove. "The timer. I was checking the oven timer."

He chuckles. "Uh huh." He shuffles up beside me and brushes against me as I continue rolling. "Just tell me when I can start pressing."

I turn to him, all flirtatious. "Haven't you been doing that since you got here?"

"Cookie cutters, Maria." He laughs. "I'm talking about making cookies."

"Oh." I feel silly. "Go ahead." I pick up my rolling pin. "But be careful. I have a rolling pin, and I'm not afraid to use it."

We spend the next few hours baking. Daisy's kitchen is small, but it serves its purpose. The air fills with the wonderful smell of sugar cookies, my favorite. In between, I get out the ingredients for the homemade frostings. I like to have more than one flavor. I dip my finger in and suck the sweet from it, testing to be sure I got it right. Nick's beside me in a flash.

"Let me taste." His eyes are glued to my finger.

I turn away to the sink. "Dip your own finger in."

He grabs my hand, dips my finger in the bowl, and licks just the tip. The kitchen just got a whole lot hotter. I have no words. I might have temporary aphasia.

"Tastes pretty good." He licks his lips.

I cough and give him a shove. "You're such a perv."

"Hey." He throws his hands up. "I'm just tryin' to be a good baker. I'm just tryin' to learn." He lays it on thick.

I can't help it, and I start laughing. "Well, the first thing you need to learn about baking is how to clean up a mess. You can wash the dishes."

He hip bumps me and looks all wounded. "I thought we'd wash them together. You know, a team effort."

I look around at the piles of cookies covering all the countertops and the kitchen table. "Sheesh. Daisy sure made a lot of dough. What is she going to do with all these cookies?"

Daisy pops around the corner and startles me. "I'm sending them to your little juvie friends down at the L. J. Youth Center."

Nick laughs. "Juvie friends? Do tell."

"They're not all juvie kids." I sigh. "Besides, juvie kids need love and kindness too."

"A girl after my own heart." Nick pats his chest. "I knew you'd look for the good in everyone." He winks at me. "I was a bit of a juvie kid."

I nod. "Why does that not surprise me?"

"Whoa." He pouts. "What's with all the judging?"

"Here." I hand him the bowl. "That's not judging. That's a fact. I've got three different frostings and a bunch of bare cookies. Let's get to work, Juvie." I give him a wink.

Nick starts on one set of cookies. His head pops up. "Hey! Do you have any sprinkles? Cause I love sprinkles! Especially the shiny, sparkly kind."

"Yes." I laugh out loud at his boyish charm. "The sprinkles are up in that cupboard. Sprinkle away."

Chapter Twelve

Baking sugar cookies makes the night pass too fast. Today closes in on me. Tomorrow it's back to work. Usually, I like working three twelve-hour shifts and being off for four days. But now that Joy is here, I would love a shorter workday. I sit on my bed and massage my face. I will my relaxation mode to kick in. Someone's knocking on my door again, interrupting my thoughts.

"Yes." Please let it be anyone but Nick.

Daisy rushes into my room and tosses the newspaper on my bed. I turn to face her, wearing my facial cleansing mask.

"Oh! You gave me a start!" She places her hand over her heart. "You and your weird cleansing rituals." She puts a hand over her heart. "You look like an alien."

I roll my eyes. "Did you need something?"

"Oh, yes. I was reading through the paper. There's an ad for a school nurse. And these so seldom come open, and it's right here, in our town. You would have daytime hours. I can't help but think it's providence! And I might even know someone on the inside. You know what they say. It's all about who you know."

"Thank you, Daisy." I answer her carefully. "Thanks for the heads up, but I wouldn't get too excited. I mean, even if I decide to apply, lots of people will probably be going for it. You can't beat that schedule."

"Well. I think you should go for it! You've been working long days, and I think you'd be happier to be on a different schedule. That's my two cents anyway." She puts her hands on her hips. "You never know until you try."

As soon as she leaves the room, I run next door to the bathroom sink to wash my face. That done, I grab my laptop so I can start the online application process for the school nurse job. What Daisy said is true; it never hurts to have options. I dash down the dark hallway, trip on a cord, and go flying, just as Nick steps into the hallway. I hit him like a clumsy linebacker. There's a shattering of glass as he falls backwards into the China closet at the end of the hallway.

"Son of a bitch!"

"Nick!" I throw my hand over his mouth. "Don't swear in front of Joy!" I feel a wet licking of my fingers. "Gross! Why?"

He laughs, while he groans at the same time, holding the back of his head, sitting on his butt, leaning forward. "Joy is with Dale in the chair. She can't hear me clear back here. It's a wonder you didn't knock me clean out. I think I hit my head on that damn thing. I might even be bleeding."

I pick myself up off the floor and hold my hand out to him. He ignores it. He sits up on his knees. I flip the light on in the room nearest to him. "Nick. You're right, you're definitely bleeding." I grab his tee shirt and pull it up his back to soak up the blood running down his neck.

"Yeah, I figured as much. The only question is where?"

"I'm not sure. I think you'd better come in the bathroom under the light. Let me look you over." I feel so awful. I can't believe I ran him into the glass.

"Why didn't you just say so?" He grabs the side of the

doorjamb and pulls himself up off the floor. He wobbles a little. He walks ahead of me, and I can't help but notice the bloodstain on the back of his tee shirt grows bigger as I keep it in place. I follow him into the bathroom and shut the door.

"I'm taking off your shirt."

"Yes, ma'am." He starts to help me but stops mid motion. He staggers a little and bumps into the wall. He leans on it. "Whoa."

"Just sit down here." I put the lid down. "Sit down. I'll get your shirt off." I tug his shirt over his head and reapply it to his bleeding head. "Do you think you can hold this here to slow the bleeding?"

"Why can't you?" His response is an incoherent groan attached to a shaking hand as he leans into his wadded-up shirt.

"Um...you've got glass in your back." His free hand flies toward his back. I swat it down with my free one. "Don't touch it! That'll make it worse."

He puts his hand on his thigh. "Well. Get the glass out."

I sigh. "Are you sure you don't want me to take you to the hospital? It looks like there's quite a bit in there."

He turns his head towards me slightly. "You want to drive me to the V.A. Hospital clear across town this time of night when you work in the morning? You could just clean me up yourself. I trust you."

Have mercy. That's a lot of glass. "I can do it. It's just going to sting."

He touches the back of my leg. "You got some whiskey in the house?" Whiskey and Nick in a small, enclosed space. This is a terrible idea.

"I think I can find something. I'll be right back."

Despite everything, he laughs. "I'm not going anywhere."

I nod before running to the kitchen to get two shot glasses, Dale's bottle of Jack Daniel's, and a can of coke.

Dale shoots me a grin. "Shots this time of night are never a good idea, Maria."

I turn to him in explanation. "I knocked Nick over in the hallway and he ran into the China closet. He's got some glass in him. I've got to get it out. There's also glass in the hallway, on the floor. I'll clean it up. Just stay away from the China closet."

Dale laughs out loud. "So…he really was a bull in a China closet."

"Dale! Now's not the time for jokes. Nick may have a concussion."

"Lighten up, Maria. He's a soldier. I'm sure he's seen worse." He waves his hand at me. "Run along and tend to your patient. I'll make sure Daisy knows."

I hand Nick the whiskey in a glass before pouring my own. He clinks my glass with his. "To bravery." We down our drinks. He bares his teeth a minute and looks up at me. "Make sure you get it all."

I wash my trembling hands, reminding myself I do this kind of thing all the time. I get out the tweezers and soak them in alcohol. Nick turns sideways to lean over the tub, grabbing Daisy's support bars. I wonder how long it will be until I no longer envision his broad back stretched out over the tub. I lean over him and pull out the glass with the tweezers as quickly and painlessly as possible. I hate myself more with every shard I remove. I feel his quick intakes of breath with each piece. I quit counting after the tenth piece, and it's a relief when I'm finally done. I get a cold washcloth and apply firm pressure to staunch the bleeding in the deeper wounds. Nick's absolutely silent and I almost wish he would say something, as the only movements I hear are his shallow breaths.

I clean the wounds and pat them dry and apply triple antibiotic ointment. I hunt around until I find the first aid kit that has paper tape and gauze. I manage to cover all his wounds. "Alright, Nick. That part is done. Turn and face me. I need to check your pupils. I'm worried you have a concussion." He sits up slowly and faces me. I glance at his front and try not to salivate over his chest and abs. He downs another shot and looks up at me with a silly grin on his face.

"Stop gloating, Nick. I'm checking to see if you have any glass on the front of you." My words are harsh, but I can't take his face.

He moves his pecs at me. "Go ahead. Look all you like."

I take my trusty pen light and flash it right in his eye with no warning.

"Ah, man. That's bright. What was that for?"

"I'm checking your pupils to see if they're fixed. I have to shine the light. Your eyes are almost as dark as your pupils. Look up here again, please." He stares up at me, but we're almost eye to eye. I shine the light a few more times until I'm satisfied. "Your eyes look good. Can you show me where you hit your head?"

He feels the back of his head with his hand and stops on one spot. "Right here, I hit it right here. It's really tender. Please be careful."

I try to see but can't. It's on the top of his head, near the back. "Lean forward." He leans forward. His head practically rests between my breasts. I try to ignore this fact as I run my hands lightly over his head of thick hair. I feel the bump. "You've definitely got a goose egg, but I think it's done bleeding. Good thing it's sticking out, that's better than growing the other way; that would be more of a concern. Now, hold still because I need to clean the wound."

I wash as gently and quickly as possible.

He leans into me and lays his head on my chest. "I need a pillow."

I smack his shoulder lightly and push him away. "I'm not a pillow!"

He pouts. "Well, then, how about a kiss to make it better?"

I reach over and down another shot of whiskey before

taking his face in my hands and kissing the crown of his head. Once I start, I can't stop. I tilt his head back and kiss his eyebrows, and all along his arresting jawline that drives me completely crazy. I know I'm playing with fire as I close my eyes and place the softest of kisses on his beautiful lips; the lips that have been haunting my dreams. It's so easy to sink into him and get lost for a little while. I'm getting all steamed up, when there's a knocking at the door. I pull myself away from him.

I clear my throat. "Yes?"

Dale coughs on the other side of the door. "Little miss is ready for bed, and so am I."

"Of course. Just lie her down on my bed, please. I'll be there in a second. Thanks."

I turn back to Nick. "You'd better get some rest. I've got to go; I've got a long workday tomorrow."

He grabs my hand and holds it up to his lips, then drops it. "Thank you for taking care of me."

I'm all sorts of flustered. "Well, it's the least I could do. I kind of knocked you into the China cabinet."

Dear Diary,

I'm back. I suppose it's not the worst thing Nick is staying here. I mean, maybe he can get to know Joy better, and that's what I intended, right? I'm not sure. I felt like it was the right thing to do, but I never anticipated that he would be such a temptation. I've got to try harder to keep my distance, as every time I turn around, he's right there.

I think the best thing to do for now is be his friend. It'd be wiser and less messy, and I do want to get to know him better. I don't want to lose Joy, and it looks like they might be a package deal. It's too early to tell. I mean, what if he's an impulsive guy, and acts on whims? What if he decides he can't commit to her or me? How will I know if he can follow through? Joy is my priority. I can't afford to lose my head over his good looks. Joy deserves a level-headed caregiver, and I'll do anything for her.

Goal: Keep my focus on Joy and off of hot soldier boy.

-Maria

Chapter Thirteen

My alarm goes off three times before I manage to drag myself out of bed to face the day. I remember vaguely someone coming in and then my bed was colder. I take a quick shower and braid my wet hair sloppily in my hurry to get ready for work. I throw on a pair of scrubs and head to the kitchen. The coffee's already on? What's Daisy doing up this early? I come around the corner. Nick stands at the stove. He's cooking something that smells heavenly. He glances at me. "Morning. Come eat."

I nod dumbly, walk over to the table, and sit down. "Where's Joy?"

He tosses the kitchen towel over his shoulder, moseys over, and nudges my leg with his as he leans over. He smells all manly and freshly showered. He scrapes some eggs onto my plate.

I pinch myself to be sure I'm not dreaming up a gorgeous Folgers coffee man from a faraway lala land in the mountains with chirping birds who randomly stepped into my kitchen and made my breakfast like he lives to serve me. "I'm sorry what?"

"I *said* I left her in Daisy's bed about thirty minutes ago.

Thought you might like some breakfast. I'm a light sleeper and your alarm woke me."

I smile up at him. "Can't say I'm sorry about that."

He throws his head back and laughs. He heads for the coffeepot and brings me a cup, adding milk to it just like I like. He grabs his own cup and sits down across from me.

I know it isn't wise, but I allow myself a little daydream and imagine having breakfast every morning with Nick and little Joy. Wouldn't that be nice? Who am I kidding? Guys like Nick don't look twice at girls like me. I was the last girl in my class to get invited to the prom, and it felt more like a pity date all night. And it sure didn't have an adorable baby in the equation. I was a major bookworm and class valedictorian, and those are the kinds of things that kept me home on a Saturday night.

"Why the frown?"

I snap out of it. "Come again?"

"I said, why the frown?"

"Oh. I, uh, was just thinking about things. I've got to go to work; can't be late. Thanks for breakfast." I finish my eggs in record time and start for the door.

"Maria."

I would have kept going had he raised his voice to me, but his soft, desperate whisper draws me in. I turn back. "Yeah?"

He holds out my to-go cup in his hand. "You forgot your coffee."

I reach for it, and he moves backwards, teasing me.

I shrug my shoulders. "I don't need it that bad." I should have seen it coming. I should have realized what I just said. In less than a second, I'm backed up against the kitchen wall, being held captive by his magical kiss. My cell phone alarm sounds, and he backs off, leaving me breathless.

His fingers tap the wall beside my head, and his mouth tickles the side of my ear; "My Maria. You need me. You need me bad."

I hate his cockiness, and worse, I hate the fact he's right. I duck under his arm and elbow my way out of his embrace. His hand darts out at me with the coffee cup as I head out the door. "Have a nice day."

I grab my coffee cup and squash the desire to hit him in his perfect face or toss hot coffee on his beautiful pecs. I give him a glare as I exit; silently cursing myself that I'm late and cursing Nick because he made me forget to say goodbye to Joy. The man is taking over my life and my thoughts. He's driving me insane. It won't be long and every room in my house will have a memory of him.

I've never been so relieved to get to work, to get my mind on anything besides his fiery kisses and the fact that he seems to fit inside my life so well. I've got to find a way to get distance. But how?

I manage to go through my workday and only think of Nick several times an hour. This is nuts. I know by the end of the day I must be more desperate than I realized when I'm actually considering signing up on match.com, a suggestion my friend Aubri had made to me about six months ago. I wasn't ready then, and I'm not sure I'm ready now, but I've got to do something. The shift's finally over and it's time to go home. I see tall, blond Richard waiting at his usual post. Most nights we walk out together. He's hospital security. We walk along chatting like always. I'm almost to my car when I hear a throat clearing. You've got to be kidding me. I see Richard's smile falter briefly as Nick steps into the light.

"Who's that?" Richard turns to me. "Do you know that guy? Is he giving you trouble?"

"No." I turn to Richard and squeeze his arm, thankful for his protection. "He's, well, he's a friend. It's okay, really."

Nick calls out to me, waving and smiling, but I can feel his glare from here. "Maria."

"Hey, Nick," I'm more than a little annoyed. What's he doing here? "Did you need something?"

He takes the manly power stance, feet spread apart, thumbs in his jean pockets with fingers spread wide, leaning back slightly with his chin up. “Not really. Daisy kind of sent me to get you.”

“Oh?” I’m a little concerned. “And why would she do that? Is everything okay at home?”

He gives me a small resistance-is-futile smile, and this just ticks me off more. “Yeah, everything’s fine. Are you coming then?”

I turn to Richard, wishing he would go back inside. “Thanks for walking me to my car.”

“Sure, Maria. Anytime.” His eyes won’t leave Nick’s face.

Nick clears his throat again. “Shall we go then?”

I hate feeling like a consolation prize in a game of tug-of-war between two grown men. “I’m sure I can make it home on my own just fine, Nick.”

“Yeah, probably. But it’s dark, and this parking lot isn’t well lit. Anyway, you can’t be too careful. I came to get you. Daisy sent me. I guess she got worried. I’m just the messenger.”

“A message you seem all too eager to deliver.” Richard’s voice comes out a little harsh.

“Hey.” I don’t hesitate as I lay my hand on Richard’s arm again. “There’s nothing to worry about here. Daisy’s just a bit overprotective. I’ll see you tomorrow?”

Nick’s eyes are flat and dark. He stares at my hand on Richard’s arm. It’s not much of a stretch to imagine him tearing Richard apart with his bare hands. “Come on, Maria. It’s getting late. We need to go if you want to catch Joy before her bedtime.” Nick’s voice is gruff and too much like a demand for my liking.

Oh no, he didn’t.

I turn back to Richard. “Thanks again, for walking me out.”

He looks down at me, gives me a smile, and pats my hand.

"Well. Like I said, anytime, Maria. Anytime." Richard gives Nick a one-finger salute as he walks away.

Nick starts after him, and I grab his arm at the elbow, stopping him mid-step. "Nick. Stop."

"What do you mean, stop? The man just flipped me the bird."

"Ignore it. He's just trying to get to you, and he's winning."

"What is he to you?" Why is Nick accusing me?

"He's my co-worker, not that it's any of your business. I swear, Nick. Not everyone is after one thing, just you."

"Oh, Maria." He chuckles, shaking his head. "Don't kid yourself. That man has thought about you in every way imaginable. He's just better at hiding it."

"Nick." I shudder at his words. "Whatever, Nick. You're such a perv. Not everyone thinks like you do."

He laughs as he opens my car door. "That's where you're wrong, Maria. We men are pretty simple animals. We all think the same and are happy to be led around by our…by what we want the most."

"Well, then." I gut punch him. "Thank God we women are more complex and self-controlled. You'd be lost without us."

He grins. "I completely agree. Can we go home now? Please?"

"Yes. Just let me get my keys and stop blocking my door."

He moves to the side, taps the top of my door, and checks his cell phone. He looks at me all sheepish. "Could you, uh, give me a ride home please?"

"Seriously? Where's your car?"

"Daisy gave me a ride out here. She said she felt like a drive." He ducks his head. He's a terrible liar.

"You got played by an old lady? What if I say no?"

"Well." He flashes me a smile. "Then I guess I'll just have to call her up and tell her you wouldn't give me a ride. I imagine she'll be mighty disappointed." He's all smug. This is so annoying.

"Unbelievable." Now I'm really irritated. "You're unbelievable. I can't believe you're using my elderly friends to get closer to me."

"I didn't really want to. It was her suggestion. I mean, I wanted to see you, but I was worried I would be invading your space. But you know Daisy. I hate to disappoint her, and I didn't want to shoot her down when she seemed so excited." He prattles on, despite my staring him down.

"Alright, already. That's enough." I give up. "Just get in." I smile over at him. "But you have to ride in the back."

Annoyance flashes in his face. Good. He opens the back door and taps the top of my car. "I've always wanted a chauffeur." I frown and hop into the driver's seat. Leave it to Nick to have the last word. Every time. That's usually my thing.

Nick peppers me with questions about Richard all the way home until I've finally had enough. "How many more questions you going to ask me about Richard? I mean, if you want to date him, just say so. I'll give you his number."

"You're so funny. I think we both know where my interest lies." His eyes burn me through the rearview mirror. I've never met anyone so direct.

"Nick." As much as I hate to say it, I have to. "Just because you think you want me, doesn't mean you get to have me. I just happened to be the woman who showed up with Joy. That's all. It could have been...anyone." I hate that my voice gets smaller as this conversation goes on.

"No." Nick reaches out and takes my hand. "No Maria, it couldn't have been just anyone, because not just anyone would do what you've done. Most people would have called the cops by now and left Joy with strangers and went on with their life. You didn't do that. You've gone the extra mile, and then some." His voice is filled with admiration, and I feel so undeserving. I need Joy as much as she needs me, but I'm not ready to admit it. At least not to him.

"Nick. Don't put me on a pedestal. You've met Joy. You

understand why I couldn't have done any of those things. A person who's halfway decent would have fallen half in love with her as soon as they met her."

I hear a sigh beside me. "Yeah. I know the feeling." He sounds so beaten down. What's going on here?

"Who was she?" His voice is filled with such longing. I feel his pain.

"What?" Why does he sound so irritated?

"Who was she? There must have been someone who's left you feeling so dejected."

He looks at me like I'm clueless for about half a second. "It, um, doesn't really matter. It's like you said, I need to focus on getting to know Joy better."

His evasiveness stings, but I won't let it get to me. "Good idea."

Dear Diary,

Today was a good day. It was really nice to have breakfast ready and waiting for me. As long as I live, I don't think I'll ever forget the image of Nick standing in front of the stove - frying pan in hand. Who knew cooking could be so sexy?

I never knew what it felt like to be treasured, how the single act of a man handing me a cup of coffee was the sweetest thing I've ever experienced. I know these sound like ordinary acts, but when the *right one* comes along, everything is seen in a different light. I'm definitely in over my head.

Goal: Keep my head around Nick.

-Maria

Chapter Fourteen

Three days go by faster than I thought possible. I've gotten used to breakfast with Nick way too quickly, although the days of him stealing kisses seemed to have passed. I'm not sure what to think about that. I'm grateful, as I'm finally starting to relax around him, and my walls are coming down. I'm no longer guarded, waiting with delicious anticipation mixed with dread for his next assault on my senses. His sexual prowess is on the back burner, and sometimes I almost forget his other side, except for those moments; the moments his hand rests lightly on my hip as we lean over Joy as we watch her nap. I hate the part of me that longs for his touch on my skin. Or the moments he hands me my morning coffee, and his fingers brush against mine, and there's a lingering. Or is it just wishful thinking on my part?

Day four comes, my day off, and I've never been more ready. I hop out of bed, ready to go down to the L. J. Youth Center, named after a famous Texas football player. It feels like it's been forever since I've been there. Everyone except two staff work there on a volunteer basis, so each day is different, and every working adult who shows up is an added bonus to the few who work there regularly every day. I see by the clock I didn't sleep in as much as I thought, and I still have a few hours to kill. I shower quickly, roll my long curly hair up into a knot, and band it in place, letting a few whispies hang free from my make-shift bun. I rush down the stairs in my yoga pants and long tee. Just as I expected, Nick stands at the stove, making French toast. As much as I want some, I'm trying to swear off bread. I go for a banana instead and grab a second for Joy, who's up early. She sits in her high-chair pounding away with her little fists, scattering her soggy milk-filled cheerios around.

I make quick work of chopping the banana into swallow-size pieces, then take them over to her.

Tentatively, she pokes at a piece of banana. She makes a silly face as it sticks to her finger. She waves her hand around, as if trying to shake it off. I can't help but laugh out loud as I make a video.

Quick as a flash, Nick is there with a spoon. He scoops up a piece and puts it in her mouth. She grabs onto the spoon and tries to take it from him. He takes hold of her little hand and gently scoops up another piece of banana, waiting for her to repeat the motion. "Maria. Flip my toast. I'm busy." Nick's orders flip my insides. Who knew a kitchen boss could be so sexy.

I head over to the skillet. Before too long, Joy has mastered the spoon and banana. I'm so proud! "Nick! She's such a quick learner!"

He laughs at me.

"What?"

He puts his arm around me, pulls me close, and kisses the top of my head. "Maria. You're already such a great mother."

His one statement spoken in true sincerity sucks the air from the room, and I can't do anything but nod stupidly as I go off to the bathroom to hide my tears. I silently chastise myself; it's not Nick's fault I can never have my own babies. He has no idea. The cold water splashes my face. I snap out of it. Crying calls for baking, and Daisy's convection oven cooks everything twice as fast, because I can use both racks at the same time. I head back to the kitchen determinedly. Before too long, I'm whipping up some muffins. Nick sneaks out the side door with his thick toast in hand. Good. I could use some distance from his prying eyes, roaming hands, and direct orders. Why does he have to look so good doing it?

Daisy's bright yellow kitchen fills with heavenly muffin smells and music from my phone. Joy's been a good sport so far, sitting in her highchair, playing with her plastic utensils I gave her. I watch her out of the corner of my eye, and I would swear she's watching my hands as I measure, dump, and stir. Maybe she's going to be a cook too!

Nick disappeared on me. I've come to know his presence so keenly; I think I could pick him from a line-up just by his scent. Four batches of muffins bake faster than I thought. Mid-cooking, I move Joy from her highchair to her bouncing chair hanging from the doorframe. She never tires of bouncing up and down. She seems to have Nick's restless energy. I glance at the clock and see it's about time for me to go. Nick is still nowhere to be found.

Joy comes out of her bouncy seat reluctantly. She grabs the sides as I gently pry her out. I prop her on my hip as we go searching for Nick. Is it my imagination, or is Bruno Mars coming from Daisy's greenhouse? My musings prove true as I step out the side door and cross over the threshold into what I'd been told is Daisy's sacred space; so why is Nick out here? Joy's face lights up. She claps her hands to the music as we walk through Daisy's prize-winning roses and mixture of flowers she grows year-round.

Will wonders never cease? It's like I've walked into some strange movie scene, as I see the back of Nick, all bare and glistening with sweat, which drips down into his shorts. He stands amongst the flowers, pouring a watering can. Off in the far corner, I see Daisy's Japanese screen set up, and the corner of a weight bench sticks out. I try not to feel injured; as I had asked Daisy once if I could set up an easel in her greenhouse, but she had declined, saying it was her workspace. Apparently, I'm not the only female in this house bewitched by Nick.

Nick turns to face me. His face appears so serene and angelic, he reminds me of Michael the archangel. His gaze never waivers from mine as he walks toward me through the flowers. He follows Daisy's winding path, being careful not to knock over any pots. He stops in front of me, saying nothing. The hungry look I recognize so well rests in his eyes. My gaze eats him up of its own accord, and I feel powerless to stop it. I'm a shameless hussy with a baby on my hip, angling myself toward his body to lean into him, going up on tiptoe to reach him faster. He swoops down, meeting me halfway, with an urgency that will not be denied. Minutes go by and then Nick pulls away first, as I hear a smacking sound on his arm. Joy wants his attentions too.

"Da da." My heart breaks a little at her first word being 'da da' instead of 'Ma ma', but that is all forgotten as soon as it happens, and all that remains is Joy's first word and Nick's inflated head. He's practically floating on the ceiling.

The plastic watering pot drops to the ground. He takes Joy from my arms, holds her above his head, and spins around slowly, grinning ear to ear. Her chubby little arms reach out to him, and her sweet laughter fills the air. "Come on, Joy. Say it again."

I can hardly take the emotion in the room as she smiles down at him. It's like he pulls the words from her. It's exactly as it should be, so why does it tear me up inside.

"Da da." He lowers her slowly and holds her up against his chest.

"Nick." My voice catches. "I've got to…I was going to the youth center. Can she stay with you?"

"But it's your day off." He looks at me funny. "And Joy and I are here."

"I know. But I have other obligations too. Those kids depend on me. Besides, Dale and Daisy can help you." *And I need to get as far away from you as possible. You're like a giant vacuum of need that goes both ways, and I can't take it anymore.*

"Dale and Daisy left first thing this morning. Did you not hear their RV leave?"

Panic sets in. "What?"

"Yeah. They had an urge to see the mountains, I guess. That's what Dale said last night. I thought Daisy told you."

I search his eyes. I'm not sure I believe him. This is too much to be a coincidence. I shake my head and stare at the ground. "So, Daisy left you and me alone in the house with Joy. Did you have anything to do with this?" I slowly look him in the eye.

"Seriously?" He looks at me, all wounded. "Seriously. You think I'm that hard up to get close to you, when you've made it clear that's the last place you want me to be?"

"Alright. I've got to go. Just…just please let me know if you two go out of town."

He looks at me, all incredulous. "Where would we go?"

"I don't know. Can we please have this conversation later?" There's too much on my mind. I don't turn back as I make my escape to the youth center.

Chapter Fifteen

I unfairly unload on Eva and Abby, cousins who show up at random times to volunteer. Eva laughs at me!

"What's so funny?"

"You're basically telling us you've got a hot soldier in your house who's Joy's father. He's chasing you, and you're complaining about it?"

"I know it sounds lame. But I'm just worried. I mean, how can I tell if he likes me or if he's attracted to me because of Joy."

"Think about it, Maria." Abby shakes her head. "What you're saying doesn't make any sense. If Nick didn't like you, he wouldn't be chasing you so hard. It's not his fault he met you because of Joy. I mean, it's like you said, sometimes life chooses us, and then it's up to us to make the right decision."

Abby throws my words right back at me. She's way too good at remembering every word I say. I can totally tell she's a lawyer's daughter.

"Yeah." Eva nods her head. "And it sounds like he's trying to make the right decision. Don't fault him for that. As far as his good looks go, consider them a gift, like a bonus. He can't help how he looks."

"Maria." Abby takes a bite out of a muffin. "And he just found out he's a baby daddy, and he didn't run and hide. You gotta give him credit where credit is due."

"Ugh." I cringe at her words. "Stop saying baby daddy. You know I hate that phrase."

Abby laughs out loud and holds up her muffin. "You don't like my lingo from the teen-mom shows on T.V.?"

Eva shakes her head. "You've got to stop watching those shows, Abby. Talk about drama mamas. I'm just sayin'."

Abby looks all shame-faced for about half a second. She holds up what's left of her muffin. "These muffins are awesome! You ever consider selling them?"

"Thanks." I smile back at her. "And not really. I make them for fun. I like to bake them. I just don't need to eat them."

Abby munches happily. She pauses a minute to answer. "Well. I'd love to learn how to bake like this."

"Hey." An idea forms in my head. "Do you have any friends who want to learn to cook? I mean, What if...what if we had a cooking event at the community building and then like a bake sale? And the proceeds could go to that Christmas Jars event they've been advertising on the radio."

Eva looks at me. "Christmas Jars?"

"Yeah, you know. Like the movie. Someone puts out Christmas jars of money anonymously at people's houses who could use a little extra cash during the holidays."

Eva looks at me again. "Are you serious? This is a real thing?"

I'm losing my mind. I swear I smell Nick in the room. "Yes. It's a real thing." There's the deep voice I've come to know so very well. Unbelievable. This guy's going to follow me everywhere. I turn in his direction. He's already hanging Joy's bouncy chair in a doorway off to the side of the room.

"Nick. What are you doing here?"

"Oh, you know. I thought since you ran out, we'd come to you. Plus, it's good for Joy to see you volunteering."

I roll my eyes. "Nick, she's six months old. She won't remember today."

"Maria." He shakes his finger at me and winks at Abby and Eva who grin ear-to-ear. "Good habits never start too early with *the children*. Besides, I'd love to help. You have anything heavy lifting that needs done?" He flexes his biceps one at a time.

Eva and Abby laugh at Nick's clowning. I turn back to catch the girls smirking at each other, before glancing back at Nick's face. I know Abby snapped a pic of the two of us from across the table. I shoot her a look, which she pointedly ignores as she pockets her phone, feigning innocence.

Abby and Eva run away from the table, heading over to see Joy.

"Nick." I lower my voice. "You can't just keep following me around."

"I'm not." He makes an exasperated face at me. "I'm volunteering, just like you. I meant what I said, it's good for Joy to be here. She's not hurting anything. And it's never too young to learn good citizenship."

"Fine. I give up." I throw my hands up. "Stay if you want to. We're working on an idea. Abby showed interest in learning to bake, so I thought Daisy could give local kids a cooking lesson or two at the community center. We could have a bake sale, and then the proceeds could be given back to people in the community who could use it, like the Christmas Jar project I heard about on the radio."

"Maria." Nick stands here, staring at me. "That's amazing. How do you think of these things?"

"I didn't really think of it, Nick." I'm embarrassed. "It was more of a collaboration. I guess there's a movie out about the Christmas Jars project. I heard it on the radio the other day, and it's been on my mind ever since because I thought it was really cool! Anyway, it doesn't matter whose idea it was, what matters is putting the plan into action. We're already halfway through November."

He grabs my hand and gives it a squeeze. "I want to help." He snaps his fingers and points at me. "You and Daisy book the community center, and I'll get the word out. I might know a little something-something about computer graphics and pamphlets, and I'll bet you dollars to donuts those two tricksters do." He nods toward Abby and Eva. "And I don't know. Maybe Thomas and I can help out with the bake sale. After all, you seem to think we draw a crowd."

"Ooh!" I clap my hands with excitement. "I love it! Soldiers will definitely help with publicity. And, yes, I'll totally use your face to draw people in." I flash him a smile. "How'd you like to help with the actual baking event?"

He raises his eyebrows. "You're going to trust blonde Thomas in the kitchen. With a stove. And fire."

I make a face at him. "Should I not trust Thomas?"

He scratches the back of his neck. "Let's just say that five of us passed the detonator test in the simulation room, and one of us did not, because he got overly excited about a possible explosion and kept getting his wires crossed."

I nod my head in understanding. "Thomas likes explosions."

"Yep. You could say that. If anything is highly flammable or explosive, Thomas has a knack for finding it first. He's a natural radar for any kind of heat and disaster."

I look at Nick. "Well, we could use Thomas as a greeter or someone to draw in the crowds. He certainly has a pretty face." Nick flinches, and I can't help but giggle.

"I guess. I mean, he's alright if you like air-headed McGyvers who can start fires with broken glass and a few weeds. On accident." Nick's face is red. He's jealous.

I can't believe it. Thomas is pretty, but he doesn't do anything for me. I seem to go for dark eyes, dark hair, and a fiery temper to match.

I laugh. "I think you and Daisy can handle Thomas in a kitchen. I'll call him up."

He pulls my hand to his chest and gazes into my eyes. "On one condition, Maria."

"Oh? What's that?"

"I get to take you on a date."

No. That's a terrible idea.

I swear my knees just wobbled a bit. "Okay. When Dale and Daisy return."

Eva and Abby are back. Eva smiles at me with her ornery grin as she turns to Nick. "Abby and I can babysit Joy. I have plenty of experience with babies."

Nick winks at them and turns back to me. "There you go. We've got two babysitters. Problem solved."

Great, just great. I can't even buy myself some time. "I guess it's a date then." I mutter.

"Don't sound so excited." He looks a little dejected. Too bad. He shouldn't have strong-armed me into going out.

"Whatever, Nick. You practically blackmailed me into this date with you. What will we be doing?"

He nudges my shoulder. "It's a surprise. You need something to look forward to." I suppress a groan.

"Nick. I don't like surprises."

"That's not true. You love Joy. And she was definitely a surprise."

"She's a person, not a surprise. And there are always exceptions." I'm such a whiner. Why can't I stop?

"Who's to say I won't be an exception? You'll just have to trust me."

I give a small snort. "That's what I'm afraid of."

Roman struts up to the table. "Dang, girl. Ease up. You're being awfully hard on this guy." He sticks his hand out. "Whaddup, I'm Roman."

Nick shakes his hand. "I'm Nick." He turns to me and

smiles. "See, Maria. Roman thinks you should give me a chance."

"That's because Roman doesn't know how you..." I'm not about to finish this sentence in front of my audience, and Nick knows it.

"Because I what...Maria?" He looks back at me. His eyes have this devious twinkle.

"Oh stuff it, Nick. Why don't you go back in the warehouse and find something heavy to lift?"

Roman knocks on the table. "Actually, that's not a bad idea. I remember a project they wanted done last week, but I needed some help that wasn't here." He turns to Eva and Abby, who fold clothes and act like they're not listening to everything Nick says. "Ladies."

Nick turns to me. "I guess that's my cue." He walks out behind Roman. It takes all my willpower not to watch the back of him as he leaves.

Eva's eyes get wide. "Maria. You're in trou-ble...that man is smokin' hot."

Abby nods her head. "Yeah, I have to agree. And he's thoughtful too. I don't know, he might be a keeper."

I answer quietly. "That's what I'm worried about." We start talking about the bake sale, and that's when I remember I need to make a phone call. I step outside to call Daisy about my plans. She loves the baking fundraiser idea and tells me they'll be back in a week. I've got more to say. "Daisy. Why'd you leave me alone with Nick?"

She laughs. "Oh, Maria. Sometimes the best lessons are learned by sinking or swimming; and I don't think you'll drown. If you're going to be Joy's mama then you need to learn to trust yourself more, and you can't do that if I'm always there. Anyhoo...Dale got the traveling urge, so away we went. We'll be back soon."

I head back inside and get back to work. Roman walks

back in and hands me a bunch of one-dollar bills. "Roman. What's this?"

"Oh. I sold your muffins to the warehouse guys."

"I didn't bake those to make a profit."

"Maybe not, but they paid up." His eyes light up. "Hey! This could be the start of your community project, Christmas Jars. Every little bit helps."

My heart warms. I can't believe how fast things are coming together. "You're exactly right. Thank you."

Eva and Abby take turns entertaining Joy. She's a great sport through all of it. By mid-afternoon, she's curled up on her blanket in her playpen, sleeping next to one of Nick's hoodies, clutching the sleeve, holding it up to her cheek. Watching her rest tugs at my heart strings. There's no way I can ever let her go. What am I going to do? I look away and catch Nick's contemplative gaze across the room. How will I survive a date with this man?

Dear Diary,

Part of me is super excited about this date tonight with Nick; another part, the part that makes me want to guard my heart – is terrified. I've never met a man who makes me feel half of what he does. Sometimes he gets me so hot, I feel like I'm on fire. Other times, he's so arrogant I want to punch him below the belt.

I can't believe everyone loved my idea! It was a suggestion, but now, it's happening. How cool is that? We're having a community project and it's going to be Awe-some!

Goal: Focus on project more and Nick less (stay fully clothed on our date).

-Maria

Chapter Sixteen

Eva and Abby make themselves at home at the house. Nick slips them some money, and I pretend I don't see. I take them to the kitchen, and we go over everything again. Abby interrupts.

"Maria. You just told us all of this. It'll be fine. If we need anything, we'll text or call."

"Okay. Well, no answering the door. No one should be stopping by."

Eva smirks at me. "I promise not to take any candy from strangers."

Nick nudges me towards the front door with his hand on the small of my back. "Maria. I'm sure they've got everything under control. Besides, there may or may not be surveillance cameras set up in every room of this house." He moves his eyebrows up and down.

Abby and Eva look at each other. "Are you serious?"

"No." He laughs. "That would be cra-zy. But there is a camera over every outside door. So, I'll know whoever comes in and out of this house. And all the windows have security alarms on them. Joy's safety and security is very important to me."

We leave the house, and I hate that I have no idea where we're going. I head for my Honda Fit.

"Nope." Nick steers me away. "Tonight we're taking the truck."

I haul myself up into his big black truck, grateful I'm wearing slacks and a sweater and not a dress.

We pull up to a miniature golf course. "Nick. It's kind of cold, don't you think?"

He sighs. "Come on, Maria, be a sport. Please."

He comes around, opens up my door, and takes my hand as I climb down. He reaches into his lockbox in the back of the truck and pulls out gloves and hats. We go inside the sandwich shop. The man makes a face at us when we tell him we want to play miniature golf. "But it's freezing outside."

"I know." I turn on Nick with a satisfied smirk. "That's what I told him."

"C'mon, man." Nick leans on the counter. "What's it going to hurt? You want to lose our business or don't you?"

"Suit yourselves." He gets out two golf balls and clubs.

We step back outside. Nick stands back. "Ladies first."

I turn to him. "Fine. But this is officially speed golf. I'm not freezing my butt off out here waiting for the perfect shot." Soon we're swinging away, running around, and laughing like two teenagers. The last hole comes up, and we both go for it at the same time. I knock his ball out of play. I hit mine in first and raise my club in the air in victory, whacking him square in the face.

His hand flies to his eye and I rush over to him.

"Oh, Nick. I'm so sorry. Let me see it."

He moves his hand. The corner of his eye is already swollen. "Dang, Maria. Sometimes I think you're trying to kill me."

"I'm just a klutz, I guess. You seem to have that effect on me." I can't believe I hit him in the eye with the club!

He chuckles. “Should I be flattered or buy full body armor?”

I swat at his chest. “You’re so funny. Come on, let’s go find some frozen peas.”

We take our stuff back inside and get a wide-eyed look from the man when he sees Nick’s eye.

I lead him back to the truck, and he climbs in the passenger side. He hands me the keys. I drive a few blocks and pull into the lot. “I’ll just run in the grocery store quick. I’ll be right back.” I get back to the truck. He’s staring out the window with his one good eye. I’m such an idiot. “Nick. I’m sorry I ruined our date night.”

He looks over at me, takes the peas from my hand, and holds them to his face. “You didn’t ruin anything. And we aren’t going home.”

“We’re not? I mean, you have a black eye. You can’t go in a restaurant looking like that.” What is Nick saying? How hard did I hit him?

He chuckles. “Well, I could. But I’d rather not. Now, where would you like to eat?”

I can’t believe this guy. “I’m not choosing, especially after I gave you a black eye. You choose.”

“Fine. How do you feel about a fruit and cheese plate?” What is he talking about?

“That sounds really good.”

“I found a new place right off of Commercial.” I follow his driving directions and end up in front of a little awning. It’s a gourmet winery I’ve never heard of. Intriguing. I go to get out. He takes my arm. “Please. Allow me.”

I stop. I remind myself I agreed to this date. Minutes later, Nick’s back with a basket and two plastic cups. I’m more curious than ever.

I’m driving again.

“Have you ever been to the lookout point?” Nick’s question throws me.

I frown. "Don't you mean the make-out point?"

"It's the highest point in this town. I hear it's really pretty at night. We can look down on all the lights of the town. It should be great for stargazing."

And lots of other things that have nothing to do with looking at the night sky. I know I shouldn't agree to this.

"Alright. You've convinced me. But you stay on your side of the truck."

He laughs. "Scout's honor, Maria. If that's what you really want." He reaches over and runs his finger over the top of my hand, drawing circles.

I tighten both hands on the steering wheel.

We ride in silence.

"So. How many siblings do you have?" Nick's forced pleasantry is a tad annoying, but I'll play along. Anything is better than sitting in silence and wondering what he's thinking.

"I just had the one half-sister, Liz. How 'bout you?"

"I'm the fifth child of my parents. They had seven altogether."

Whoa. "Seven! Where are they now?"

"Scattered. I hear from my siblings here and there; none of them regular. We grew up in the heart of a kind of gangland in California. When I got old enough, I joined the army. It was either that or join a gang, and I wasn't doing that. I lost two of my brothers to that kind of life."

That's heavy.

I'm at a loss for words. I can't imagine. "Nick. I'm so sorry. I, um. I had no idea."

"That's alright. It's not your fault. How could you know?"

"So did your parents…did they move?"

"Nah. They're still in the same place. My dad can be a stubborn man. They're pretty quiet and they keep to themselves. And I think my mom can't leave the city where her sons are buried."

The sorrow in his voice makes me want to cry. Losing my

sister to illness was hard, but I can't imagine how I'd feel if someone killed her. I feel inadequate, and I don't know what to say.

"My parents have been gone a while. They, um. They died in a car wreck. Drunk Driver. I had just turned eighteen, and Liz was twenty-two. And then it was just Liz and me. But then she got sick, and so now…" I clear my throat and try to talk. "Now it's just me. Well. Me and Joy I guess." I hope. I stop at the top of the hill and put the truck in park. I steal a glance at Nick. Can't he tell how much Joy means to me? Can't he see how much I need her? He's a man. He still has plenty of time to meet someone to have children with, but that someone isn't me.

He reaches out and squeezes my hand. "Maria. You've got me too. I'm here for you. Stop acting like you're all alone."

I hate my self-preservation instinct that takes over. "You say that now. But, forever's a long time, Nick. You're used to being free and unattached. If you have a family, you can't just take off and leave when you feel like it." I want to take my words back, but I can't. Besides, I don't think he's thought everything through.

"Maria! That's not fair. You're making assumptions for me. Why do you keep assuming the worst?"

I answer quietly. "I have to. Being prepared lessens the blows." We sit in silence for a while. Nick opens the bottle of wine. He's pours it into our plastic cups.

"I'd say this conversation calls for a little wine and cheese." His attempt at humor is a perfect icebreaker, and it's appreciated.

I can't help but laugh. I reach out and take the cup from his hand. I dig into the basket and spread out our little cheese and fruit party across his big dash.

He shares some favorite childhood memories with me, and I share some of mine. We sit here in the truck, munching on cheese and fruit, drinking our wine. I roll down the window and look out at the stars. It's quite romantic. Nick's full of surprises! Clean up is quick. He hops out of the truck and spreads a blanket over the big truck's hood. He motions to me with a crook of his finger. I know there's trouble waiting for me outside, but I get out anyway.

I climb up the front of his truck to sit beside him and look up at the stars. He scoots over toward me and doesn't stop until he's flush up against me. "They say body heat is good for the cold."

I snort. "Maybe so. We could just get back in the truck."

"Where's the fun in that? Besides, the view is so much better out here." I feel his gaze on my face.

"Nick. The view's up there." I point to the starry sky.

"Maria. I know what I find beautiful."

Any more of this, and I'll never be able to keep him at arm's length. "Nick. You've got to stop with all your romantic gestures and flowery words. They may be second nature to you, but I'm not used to them. And I can't take it. I can't take another heartbreak." His pounding on the truck startles me. "What was that for?"

"You're so hard to take, Maria! Why do you assume everything I say to you is just another line? Did it ever cross your mind that you're the inspiration for my words? Would you believe me if I told you I've never talked to any woman how I talk to you?!"

"Nick. Try to understand. You're...you're so smooth. I swear romance is like your second language. I don't know how much I believe."

"Believe me, Maria. Why would you not?" He hops off the truck and paces back and forth. "All I've ever done since we met is compliment you and tell you how I feel. And all you do is find fault in what I say. You're un-believ-a-ble!"

"I'm sorry, Nick, but I'm a realist. I know you can't help the way you look, but it makes you harder to trust. You've got to see that." I know I sound lame and repetitive, but I don't know what else to say.

He stops in front of me. "So if you thought I was less attractive, you'd be more inclined to believe me? What sense does that make? I mean, by your measures, I shouldn't trust you to walk out the front door without laying down with every single guy you meet."

"Nick! Really? Do you need to be so crude?"

"Am I? That's basically what you're implying about me. You're insinuating that since I look like this, I'm a player. You think I'll say anything to get a woman into bed! How long are you going to hold my looks against me? I just want to be with you. It's that simple."

As usual, I don't know what to say. "Nick. We've talked about this. I'm here for Joy. We need to do what's best for her. Please take me home. I need to go home."

He turns away from me and takes a deep breath. He steps up to the truck and hops back up to sit beside me. "We'll go soon. I just want to sit here, with you, and enjoy this night." He takes my gloved hand in his and tugs it up to his chest. We sit there a while. The wind starts to blow, and the cold cuts through me. I start to shiver all over. I hide from the wind and bury my face in his neck.

"Maria. Your nose is cold. What are you doing?"

I speak into his neck. "I'm freezing, Nick, and you won't let me sit in the truck, so."

"Maria, forgive me." His words cut me off. He slides down the front of his truck and drags me down behind him. He pins me against the grill, whips off his gloves, and shoves them in my back pockets. He pulls me as close as a second skin. I whip my head up in protest, which is a huge mistake, as I feel his predatory stare on my lips. All coherent thought is gone as he descends. My whole body is on fire, and it goes on and on.

Nick steps back, and I feel a little satisfaction when I see him trembling. I go to reach out to him, and I trip over my own feet, landing on my butt. He leans over towards the ground. His hands grip his thighs.

"Nick. Are you okay?"

He stands upright. Wordlessly, he sticks out his hand and I take it. He pulls me up with ease, as if I weigh less than a feather. He jerks me toward him once more and bruises my lips with his assault. "Maria. This isn't over. There's something between us. And it has nothing to do with Joy. We have a connection, and I've never felt this way about anyone. Ever. Not even close. I want you. And I'm not stopping until you're in my bed."

His words flip my insides all kinds of sideways. I strike out in self-defense. "That line might work on others, Nick. But it won't work on me. We've got chemistry, there's no doubt. But I don't give anything unless I want to. That choice is mine, not yours. I don't owe you anything. Get in the truck, or don't. I'm going home."

He whips the keys from his pocket and slams them into my hand.

I hop in the truck. Nick stands outside for a good five minutes with his back to me. His fists clench and unclench. He goes around to the back of the truck. What in the world is he doing now? I feel a shaking at the back of the truck. I glance in the rearview mirror to see Nick's veins popping in his neck, as he throws his head back with a primal yell. That sight should disgust me, not turn me on. I must be going crazy.

He climbs up in the truck, silent and pouting, and tosses a little white box at me. Even though I'm furious with him, I'm curious. I open it up. "Ooh. Chocolate-covered strawberries." I take one out and take a big bite. Deliciousness. He smacks my hand, and the strawberry goes flying across his truck.

"What the heck, Nick?!"

He growls at me. "Stop making love noises over a strawberry!"

I turn to glare at him. "You're crazy! You're acting like a

desperate, sex-starved man. Get your mind out of the gutter. You gave me the strawberry, so I ate it."

I put the truck in reverse, floor the gas, and spread gravel all around. I stomp on the brake as I see a tree pop up in my rearview mirror, but it's too late. There's a loud bang. I put it in park and jump out to assess the damage. The truck rests against the tree trunk. I look up at Nick and wait for the admonishment that should be coming any minute. He says nothing. He goes around to the truck and starts it up again and pulls forward. "Hey! You can't just leave me here!"

The truck stops as quickly as it had started. He stands beside me, holding a flashlight. "I can't see the back of the truck if it's up against the tree. You really think I'd leave you out here?"

I can't believe the hurt in his voice. "No. I just…we had some pretty awkward moments is all."

"Maria. No matter how mad you make me, I wouldn't leave you out here all alone. What kind of man do you think I am?" He hands the keys back to me and goes back to the passenger side.

I go back to the driver's side window and peer in. "There's a pretty good dent in the back of your truck."

"It still runs. Now come on. Joy's probably wondering where we are, and Abby and Eva are probably thinking I got lucky tonight. Boy, are they wrong." He's in full-on pout mode.

"I'm sorry I ruined our date." I try to sound sincere.

"No. I don't think you are."

I should keep my mouth shut, but I always have to get the last word. "I guess you're right. If you were planning on sleeping with me then I'm not sorry I ruined your night."

He says nothing in reply, just reaches out and turns on the radio.

Chapter Seventeen

We get to the house. Abby and Eva sit on the couch, playing on their phones. Joy's light snoring sneaks out from the corner playpen. Abby turns to us.

"Oh, hey. We laid her down in the living room, because we didn't feel comfortable letting her sleep where we couldn't see her," she whispers.

I glance at Nick, but he won't look at me. I turn back to Abby. "Well, we're home, so I guess you can go."

Nick clears his throat. "Let's go, girls."

I watch them walk towards the front door. "Thanks for watching Joy."

Eva turns and smiles. "No problem." They follow Nick out the door.

I scoop up Joy and head to my bedroom to lie down. I get as far as stripping down to my silk cami and matching underwear. I'm ashamed to realize a small part of me was hoping for more action. Why else would I have worn this underneath? I remember the strawberries. Nick was such a jerk to me tonight. I deserve this one consolation prize. I race to the fridge and grab them and dash back to my room. I lay down with the box resting on my chest. I take them out, one at a time, and savor each scrumptious little nibble. I drop the stems back in the box.

I'm half asleep when I wake to a choking sound. I'm in horror as I see Joy, covered in hives! She gasps and chokes on her swollen tongue. I sprint to Nick's bedroom door, banging on it as hard as I can as I barge in.

"Nick! Nick! Please help me!" He's dead to the world. I run over and smack him on the face. "Nick! It's Joy!" He stumbles out of bed and bumps me into the wall. I run past him to my bedroom, throw on a hoodie, sweatpants, and my house slippers. I scoop Joy up and hurry to the front door. Nick honks from the truck outside. I run out and lay her on the seat. She's all wrapped up in her blanket. Her eyes tear up. She's still choking!

"Pick her up and hold on tight." He peels out of the driveway and flies down the highway.

I close my eyes and start to pray. We arrive at the ER, and I jump out of the truck and rush inside. "Please! Somebody help my baby, she's in anaphylactic shock!" The lady behind the desk takes a look at Joy and hits the alarm button. Everything after that happens so fast. She's ripped from my arms, and the doctor's asking all kinds of questions, most of which I can't answer. He administers the shot as they wheel her back. Then we wait. I'm sitting here, going over everything that could have possibly caused her reaction, and I have no idea. The doctor returns. "Excuse me. Are you Joy's parents?" I open my mouth to explain, but Nick speaks up.

"Yes, we are. Is she going to be okay?"

"I believe so, but we'd like to keep her a while longer, given her reaction. Are you either of you in the habit of giving her strawberries? We found part of one in her hand, and I believe that's what caused the reaction. Strawberries are not a food I would advise giving someone so young, especially given the extreme nature of her allergic reaction."

I fall apart at his words. "I took the strawberries to bed last night, and I thought I got them all back in the box, but I must have dropped one. And shesh…e found it…She could have died. I…I almost killed her."

Nick reaches over and squeezes my hand. "She's going to be okay, Maria. She's going to make it. It was a mistake. That's all. I'm the one who bought the strawberries. Be mad at me."

The doctor clears his throat.

"I've got to get back to my patients. One of you can go with me to her room if you'd like."

Nick looks over at me.

I can't go in there. I shake my head. "You go, Nick. I'd like to stay out here for a while."

He holds my gaze for a few more seconds. "I'll go. But promise me you'll be here when we come out."

"I promise." I pinch the sides of my legs in my nervousness. I know I'll have bruises tomorrow, but I can't seem to stop. I've had Joy less than a month, and already I'm a failure as a mother. She could have died tonight, and it would have been my fault; all because I wanted those strawberries because I was upset with Nick. It all seems so trivial now. I try to hold on to Nick's words. It was a mistake. A terrible, terrible mistake. But it was my mistake. I can't get past that. The future seems so uncertain. I thought I knew what I was supposed to do. I thought I was here to take care of Joy. But now I just don't know.

An eternity later, Nick walks out of the ER with Joy. She sleeps peacefully on his shoulder. One arm is curled next to her chin and the other hangs slack down his arm. Her dark curls I love so much cover her face. I rush over and lift her hair so I can see her cherub face. She's breathing easy. I relax a little. Nick starts to hand her to me. I shake my head again.

"No. I'll drive the truck." He goes to reach for his keys. "I'll get them." I stick my hand in his sweats pocket and dig them out.

He shifts a little after. "You have no idea what kind of dreams I'll be having tonight." His attempt at humor falls flat.

I keep walking.

"I'm sorry. I was just trying to lighten the mood."

I close my fist tight around the key until it cuts into my hand. Only then do I loosen my grip. Our drive home is silent. I'm thankful for the size of his truck as I drive down as many side roads as possible, wanting to stay off the highway. Driving slower feels safer.

We get in the house and Nick turns to me. I put up my hand. "Nick. I can't talk. Not right now."

He nods his head and stalks back to his bedroom.

I go to my room and sit on the side of my bed. The impact of what happened tonight with Joy hits me all at once. I shake uncontrollably and sink to the floor. I cover my mouth to keep from crying out. I don't want to wake Joy, and I don't want Nick's comfort. I deserve to be left all alone. How could I have been so stupid and careless?

I grab my diary and write through my tears.

Dear Diary,

I'll never forget our trip to the ER as long as I live. I had such a terrible feeling of helplessness, watching Joy fight for her breath. Thank God I woke up when I did. I'm such a careless idiot. Why couldn't Nick yell at me, just this once? His kindness was my undoing. He made good points, but all I can see is my mistake that could have been fatal. I don't know if I'm fit for motherhood, even though Nick seems to think so.

Goal: I don't have one.

-Maria

I toss my diary to the floor. My eyes well up with tears

again. All I can still see in my mind is Joy's red face, gasping and choking for air.

Nick's arms wrap around me before I even knew he was in my room. I tense up and pull away from him, trying hard to keep my walls in place.

"Maria." He holds me tighter. "Talk to me. It was just a mistake. It could have happened to any of us."

I shake my head back and forth furiously. "No, Nick. It couldn't. It didn't happen to you. It happened to me. I'm the only one selfish enough to take such a risk. Why did I think it was a good idea to take strawberries to bed with me, with her lying right there?"

"Maria. You've got to let this go. It was an honest mistake. That's all. I know you didn't intend to hurt Joy. You know it and I know it. Let it go."

"Nick. It's not that simple. I can't let it go. Don't you see I failed her? She was left in *my* care, and I messed up. I messed up big time. She could have died."

"But she didn't."

"No, she didn't. But part of me thinks she was probably better off with her real mom. At least she didn't do this to her."

"First of all, you don't know that. And second of all, she may not have taken her to the ER, but she left her on a stranger's porch! Like she was something she didn't want anymore. And it was completely intentional. What you did tonight wasn't. It was an accident. Can't you see that?"

"There's more to it, Nick. You don't know." I'm so embarrassed.

He growls in my ear. "Then why don't you explain it to me? Because I'm getting really tired of trying to read your mind."

"I haven't talked about this in a long time, and it's a part of my life I'd just as soon forget. I was married once. To a guy named Ron. We were both eighteen, young and stupid. It was a whirlwind romance. We were carefree and in love. We eloped. It wasn't long, and I was pregnant. I was so excited. That baby meant everything to me. I was six months pregnant. We had a name picked out for our baby girl, Olivia Rachel Dixon. I painted her nursery, bought a crib and diapers. Even had her coming-home outfit…but it wasn't enough. She…she wasn't meant to be—at least not for me. After…I never set foot in her nursery again. Our marriage fell apart as fast as we had gotten together. We tried to make it work, but the loss was too much.

He dragged me through genetic counseling and tried to get some kind of answer for what happened. I guess he thought it would help. And that's when we found out I couldn't carry our baby to term. I couldn't have Ron's children. And I couldn't live with that. I fell into a depression that lasted for weeks. He got tired of waiting for me to snap out of it, and I guess he couldn't live with what I'd become, because he started staying out all night, making no secret about where he'd been. That's when I knew it was over. So I left.

After working in crappy jobs for a few months, I decided to focus on something positive. I enrolled in nursing school. It was such a relief to focus all of my energy on one thing, and to take my mind off all the pain and sorrow. So, that's me. And now you know why I'm not meant for motherhood." I sit here, squeezing my hands together in my lap, too embarrassed to look him in the eye after baring my soul to him.

Nick sits beside me. He's quiet for what feels like the longest time. I think he finally gets it. "Maria. I'm sorry you went through all of that. I truly am. But it doesn't mean you're not meant to be a mom. Maybe you didn't carry Joy for nine months, but you are her mother. Yes, she was in danger, but you didn't put her there. Not on purpose. You did everything you could tonight to save her. Can't you see that? And I don't believe that you aren't meant to have another baby. It just wasn't your time."

"You're not hearing me. I can't have children. After my

miscarriage, we went to the doctor. He tested us. He told us in plain language we'd never have a baby. He said I couldn't carry Ron's baby to term."

He coughs. "I'm hearing you just fine. That was four years ago. And I'm not Ron."

I laugh. "Obviously."

"Maria. What I'm saying is, it might be worth checking into again. Maybe you couldn't carry Ron's child to term. But that doesn't mean you can't carry someone else's. Maybe it was your DNA together that caused the problem."

A little seed of hope has sprouted, and I want to smash it down, for fear I'll get hurt. But I can't. I want to believe Nick's words. How did I not come to this conclusion on my own? I'm a nurse. Have I really been so blinded by what I thought was my motherless fate? I turn and look him in the eye. "Nick. Why are you being so nice to me? I put your daughter in harm's way tonight. It was an accident, as you've said. But it still happened."

"Maria. I've watched you with Joy. You would never do anything to hurt her. You love her as your own. I see that. How can I not care for you, when I see how much you care for her? And now we know she's allergic to strawberries. So, the next step is to take her to an allergy doctor and get her an Epipen. We just have to be more prepared. Get some sleep. Tomorrow, Eva and Abby are coming over and we're going Christmas tree shopping."

"Nick. I don't want…" I find myself stopping mid-sentence. "I mean, that sounds really nice."

Morning comes. The smell of coffee draws me to Daisy's bright kitchen. I'm embarrassed to find the girls waiting and ready at the table in their coats and hats. Joy sits in her highchair, flinging cheerios around, grinning from ear to ear, hamming it up for her captive audience. You'd never guess she spent a night in the ER. Nick stands at the stove with his skillet, looking way too good in jeans and a sweater and in his bare feet. "Rise and shine, sleepyhead!"

Abby and Eva look over at me and giggle. Abby's phone is in her hand, and it's aimed at me.

I shoot her a look. "Abby, put that phone away if you want to live."

"Alright, alright. I take it you're not a morning person. You and my sister Isabel would get along great."

Nick turns toward the girls. "Abby. Ease up. We had a long night last night."

Eva raises her eyebrows. "Oh? Do tell."

"Gross." I clap my hands and make a face at Nick. "It's not what it sounds like. Joy had an allergic reaction to strawberries. We ended up at the ER."

Their eyes get big, and Abby answers. "Wow. Is that all over then? She must be okay. I mean, she looks okay."

"Yeah. She just gave us a big scare. That's all." Nick isn't done being ornery. "Well. Last night may not have made a big impression on Maria, but I did my best. I even took her to the lookout point to...stargaze..." He winks at me as he hands me a plate of eggs.

I walk over to the table with my eggs and coffee and go back to the fridge for the milk. I stop behind Nick to flick him hard in the back of the earlobe. His hand flies to his ear. I laugh a little. "You deserved that, Nick Laus. Shame on you for making insinuations to these young girls with their impressionable ears and wild imaginations."

"You're a cruel woman, Maria Marquez. Hurry up and eat already. We're all ready to go Christmas tree shopping."

"You could have woken me up." I shrug off his scolding. "Then you wouldn't have to wait on me. Or, just let me know where you're going, and I'll catch up to you." Then I won't have to ride with you all and your Christmas cheer this early in the day.

Eva shakes her head. "That's alright. We'll wait on you, Maria."

I sigh. "I tried." I wolf down my eggs and tell myself not to feel self-conscious, since they're all in such a hurry. I dump my plate in the sink and run down the hallway to take a quick shower. I come out to the breakfast table and brush my wet head. "Who wants to braid my hair? I love you girls' braids. Can you do one for me?"

Nick comes up behind me and grabs the brush from my hand. He places his hand on my shoulder. "I'll braid your hair."

"Oh, you're hilarious. That is not happening." Why would an ex-soldier know how to braid hair?

"You asked, and I answered first. I've got dibs." He tickles the back of my ear with his fingertip. I duck away from his hand.

"Why would you know how to braid hair?"

"I told you I had sisters growing up. Why would I not know?"

Abby whips out her phone again. "I got dibs on making a hair video by Nick."

I can't believe all this fuss over my hair. "You are ridiculous."

"Quit stalling, Maria. Let him do your hair. You asked," Eva retorts and makes a bratty face at me.

I hop up and plop down in the chair sideways. I rest my hand up on the high back. "Fine. But if I don't like it, I'm taking it out."

Nick starts brushing my hair, and I want to moan. I forgot how nice it feels to have someone else brush my hair. He runs his hands through it, and other feelings pop up, unbidden. I swat at his hand. "Get on with it then."

"I'm trying." He chuckles low. "Stop hitting me."

I look up at him. "Move fast-a."

Abby gives an overdramatic sigh and lays down her phone.

"Maria. Put your hands in your lap. Nick, shut up and get it done already. I'm gettin' old over here, and you're messin' up my future TikTok."

I roll my eyes and do as she says.

Nick salutes Abby. "Yes, ma'am." He clears his throat. "I'm just trying to figure out what I'm working with here. Chillax, everybody." He rubs his thumb over the base of my neck and digs into my scalp just enough that it feels perfectly wonderful. This has to stop.

I duck out of the way again. "I don't think you have any idea what you're doing."

He chuckles. "Believe me, woman. I know exactly what I'm doing."

Eva gets up from the table. "Get a hotel room, you two. Or stop with all the innuendos. It's embarrassing."

I side-eye her. "Thank you, Eva. I've been telling him to knock it off, but he ignores me." I reach up and pinch his hand.

"Ouch. What's with your violent nature today? First you flicked my ear and now you're pinching my hand." He tugs on my hair to get out a knot.

"I told you I'm not a morning person. Are you going to braid my hair or not?" My sharp tone feels like a teacher.

"Yes. Hold your horses."

Abby stands off to the side, making her video. I shut my mouth.

Nick's hands move quickly. Before I know it, he's halfway done. I'm impressed. "Put your head down, I can't braid the end of it if you don't."

I purse my lips together and duck my head.

"Rubber band?" He sticks his hand out.

"I don't have one. I thought they would." I look over at Eva.

"Girls?" Nick asks.

Abby sets her phone down. "I don't have one. Eva?"

"Nope. Sorry."

He's pulling on my hair. "Come on, let's go find you a rubber band."

I stand up from my chair. I'm being led around by my hair and Nick. Soon we're in my room. He digs through things on my dresser with his free hand. I reach out and grab it to make him stop.

"I'll get you a rubber band. Stop touching all my stuff." I open my drawer and pull out my plastic container. I open the lid and take out a hairband. "Here."

He spins me around. It feels strange to see him standing behind me in my mirror and playing with my hair. I look down quickly. I put my box together and put it back in its place. I know it's coming, but he still throws me off as I feel his hands on my hips. He splays his fingers wide until they're on my rib cage and moving up towards…I knock them down.

"Nick. It's time to go Christmas tree shopping."

His hands come right back to my hips again! I feel his chin on the back of my neck as he leans down to nuzzle at me. He sniffs my hair. I could just stay here.

I duck forward to get away from him and get a pair of socks from my drawer. I lean over and put them on while I'm standing. "Come on, Nick. They're waiting on us out there."

"I know, but I like it in here. Everything smells like you, all flowery and light. And I like to watch you get ready."

"Okay…" I rush over to my closet and dig through my shoes until I find my plaid winter boots. I reach up above to find a scarf, but it's way back in the corner.

"Nick?" He's behind me in an instant. "I can't reach my scarf."

He reaches up on tiptoe. I can't resist as I spin to face him. I go for his ribs and belly. His arm flies down so fast, I barely miss an elbow to the face. I look up, and his eyes are as dark as I've ever seen them. He's breathing hard. "What the hell are you doing?"

I'm laughing so hard I can hardly speak. "I…wanted… to…see…if…you…were…ticklish! Apparently not. You're kind of the opposite. Remind me to never touch your rib cage again. You look like you want to kill me right now."

"You're playing with fire, is what you're doing. Everyone has their erogenous zones, and you just found mine. I'm trying to contain myself."

"Whatever, Nick. Your erogenous zone is pretty much your entire body; and every female that looks in your general direction. It was a joke, and I was kidding. You were just so…exposed. I'm sorry…anyway, thanks for the scarf. I'll finish getting Joy ready. We'll be waiting in the kitchen for you."

I turn to go. I'm so annoyed. Nick spins me around, yanks me up against him, and kisses me senseless. It's over as fast as it started. I back away from him. "Thanks a lot. I think you left whisker burns on my chin. Now my lips are going to be all pink and swollen."

He takes my hand and tugs me toward him, whispering, "I'm sorry." He runs his hand up my arm and cradles my chin as he steps to me slowly. He leans down and leaves a whisper of a kiss on my lips. Dang it. I want more.

I turn away from him. I'm all sorts of frustrated. My closet is just one more place in my home with a memory of Nick. I'll have to hire an exorcist when he moves out.

Dear Diary,

I'll never braid my hair again without remembering his hands weaving through it, gently tugging, taking my breath away. How is every move he makes so sensual? Does every woman notice every little thing he does, or is it just me? Will I ever be able to tell the difference between love and lust?

Being around Nick is all-consuming, and lately,

resistance seems futile. He's breaking down my walls, one by one. Would it be so terrible to be wrecked by Nick?

Goal: Do not be afraid to have my heart broken, because I think it's inevitable.

-Maria

Chapter Eighteen

We pile into his big black truck. The girls climb up in the back of his king cab, with Joy between them in the car seat. "So, Nick. Where are we going for this tree?"

He smiles at the girls in the mirror as he backs out. "That's for me to know and you to find out. But I promise you, you're going to like it."

We drive and drive, passing the time playing the alphabet game, and then the license game. The girls teach us the initial game, a game of asking yes or no questions to identify famous celebrities according to their initials.

Three hours have gone by. I know where we're headed. "We're going to where you used to live. Why are we going so far away for a Christmas tree?"

"Well. We're going for the whole old-fashioned experience today. We're going to go into the woods, find our tree, and cut it down. But, we still have to abide by the law and stay off people's property. I'm not getting a ticket or a fine from someone calling the cops on me for trespassing," Nick says with a grin.

Abby speaks from the back seat. "Do we have enough time to cut down a tree with a handsaw? There's four of us, but it'll still take a long time." I can't tell if she's being serious or sarcastic.

He laughs. "I have a chainsaw. I said old-fashioned, but I didn't mean ancient." The truck grows quiet again, and Nick pops in a CD. Soon we are all singing Christmas carols.

We're like a cheesy Christmas movie, but I don't care. It's the most fun I've had in a long, long time. Soon enough, we pull up to the army base. "Nick? What are we doing here?"

"Killing two birds with one stone on our little trip. First, we do a photo shoot. It shouldn't take more than thirty minutes. It's for the Christmas Jars brochure. Shall we?"

Abby and Eva's heads pop up between us from the back seat. "We're doing it? We're taking pictures of real soldiers! Here?"

Nick turns to smile at them. "These are the barracks. This is where I spent over half my life. Let's go find some men. It's time for you two to get creative. Plus, I get to show off my daughter."

I busy myself with getting Joy out of her car seat. Nick takes off for the building. The girls look over at me, wide-eyed. "Are there *really* soldiers in there?"

I point at the sign. "Yes. This is a base."

"Bye!" They're out of the truck and running towards the building.

Minutes later, I've managed to get Joy out of her car seat. It's harder to get her out when she's all bundled up. I get her coat back on her and we head inside, as I straighten her hat on her head on the way in. A man runs up to the side of me. It's Thomas.

He wraps his arm around my waist and snuggles up to me. "Just what do you think you're doing, Thomas?"

"Messing with Nick. Play along, please."

"I have a bad feeling about this."

"Aw. It's all in good fun. Come along now."

I walk up to the building wearily, feeling like I'm somehow

betraying Nick, even though Thomas and I aren't doing anything.

Thomas steps away from me long enough to open the door, and then he's back to my side like glue.

Nick stands next to the girls by the front desk. His arms are across his chest. He stares at Thomas like he'd like to set him on fire.

What is going on here?

"Thomas."

Thomas leans over and kisses my cheek? What? He steps away from me and walks toward Nick. Thomas sticks out his hand. "Nick."

Nick ignores his hand. He punches Thomas in the face as fast as lightning. Thomas drops like a stone. Nick stands over him.

"Get up! Get up and fight me. How could you do that to me? You know how I feel about her."

I lay a hand on Nick's arm. Tension runs through him like a livewire. "Nick! Please! He was just toying with you. He told me to play along. I'm sorry. It was just…it was just a prank."

I kneel beside Thomas, who is lying on the floor…laughing? I give him a shove. "What is wrong with you?"

Thomas glances back up at Nick. His eyes are narrowed. "Payback stings, don't it, Nick."

Nick's whole face changes. "Geez, Thomas. You sure can hold a grudge. You got me, fair and square. Are we good now?"

Thomas holds out his hand. Nick takes it and pulls Thomas up off the floor, who wipes his bloody lip with the back of his hand.

Nick looks him over. "Shoot, Thomas. I was going to do some photos with you today for a benefit dinner, but I may have marred that pretty mug of yours."

I glance over at Nick. "I think we can work with it." I wink at Thomas. "Besides, aren't soldiers supposed to get a little roughed up now and then?"

Nick and Thomas run back to Thomas's to change into uniform. They return. I didn't think Nick could look any sexier, but that's because I'd never seen him in uniform. I turn around to face Abby, putting my back to Nick. "Abby. Get a pic of Nick in his uniform and send it to my phone." I turn back to face the two men. "I'm going to leave the photos up to Eva and Abby. I trust them. I think Joy and I will take a walk outside. She's been cooped up for a long time."

Nick nods his head but grabs my hand.

"Abby. Snap a picture of me and Maria and Joy."

I put on a brave face, but I tremble on the inside. This feels too much like a family photo. Why does Nick keep doing this when we're not together? It only complicates things. He gives me no time to back out. He snatches up little Joy and laughs as she goes for his hat. He turns her around to face the camera and sets his hat back in place. He reaches out and tugs me up against his side with ease. My body betrays me as it settles up against him. He sends all sorts of delicious feelings through me, as his hand grazes the skin above my hip, playing with my shirt end. I barely notice Abby taking the pictures.

The next thing I know, Nick's handing Joy to me. "Here, enjoy your walk." He gives me a wink.

I try to hide my feelings, but it's hard. Nick is determined to make me suffer. Every time I think he's done toying with my affections and respecting my boundaries; he crosses another line, and goes all hands-on again, driving me crazy. I'm about through with his games. "Abby, watch Joy a minute. I need to talk to Nick."

Nick's head pops up. He waltzes right out of the conversation I thought he was having with Thomas and a few men. "You need me?"

I almost change my mind. The huskiness of his voice waves

a huge red flag. I choose to ignore. "Yeah, I just had a question."

My mind's so frazzled, I don't even hesitate as I drag him into a closet, the first door that opens, without knowing what is on the other side. My pride gets the better of me, as he raises his eyebrows at me, challenging me. I turn the doorknob and shut the door. "Maria, what's…"

I grab him by the collar and pull him toward me as I stand on tiptoe to meet him. I dive in, headfirst, and blast through every warning sign going off in my head. I want to make Nick suffer. I want to drive him crazy, like he's been doing to me since the day I met him. I pour everything I've got into this kiss, as my hands roam over his beautiful chest and his perfect arms that always feel like home to me. His groan makes me chuckle inside with celebration. Good. Let him feel tortured. There's a calamitous sound as something loud and heavy falls to the floor. I pull away slightly, but he chases me. His kisses burn my skin like fire as he roams between my lips and my earlobes. I struggle for coherent thought. There's a knock at the door.

Nick groans again, this time in frustration. "Maria. You going to tell me what this is all about?"

"I don't know, Nick. Maybe I thought you needed a taste of your own medicine. Maybe I just wanted to drive you a little nuts with wanting me. I guess I just wanted to know if my touch gets to you as much as yours…" I stop all my whisper-talk because I've admitted too much, and that wasn't my intention.

"Of course, you get to me. Why do you think I reach out to you all the time? I need to feel you, to touch you. I've got you under my skin, and I don't see that changing anytime soon." He sounds pained.

"I'm sorry, Nick. I was just…I was just frustrated. And the family picture you had Abby take, it really hit me. Because we're not a family. We're just both here for Joy."

He hits his fist against the metal shelving, and I automatically reach for it, but he pulls away. He leans in, whispering, "Maria. Isn't that what family is? Taking care of each other, protecting each other. Being present? The fact that we're both single and have exceptional chemistry is just a bonus. Speaking of which, you dragged me in here, so I think it's only fair I get the last word."

His arms wrap around me, and he lifts me off my feet. His lips meet mine, and I go with the moment. I throw my arms around his neck and get completely lost. There's another knock at the door.

"Nick! Time's a wastin'."

My head's still spinning as he lowers me to the ground. He turns the knob, and I follow him out all hot, bothered, and embarrassed.

Loud-mouth Thomas, who doesn't miss a thing, stares at Nick. "Nick, why's your shirt untucked? Aren't we taking pictures?"

Nick punches Thomas hard in the shoulder. "Shut up, Thomas." Nick turns to me with a pained expression on his face. "Maria. Don't go too far. I want to introduce Joy around to the men." My heart pinches at the pride Nick has in his daughter.

I head out the door with Joy. We walk through the barracks. I'm fascinated by the men walking to and fro, performing their daily duties. Rules and routine definitely reign here.

Twenty minutes later, Eva and Abby run up to me. "We're done! We're supposed to bring Joy back to Nick."

"Okay. That was fast."

Abby nods. "Yeah, well, you know. They're men, and they're soldiers. They only have so much patience for taking pictures."

We walk back to Thomas's place. Thomas stands outside. He nods to the girls, then winks at me.

"Maria. Go on in. Nick's inside waiting for Joy." He says this like he's daring me.

I don't trust the look in Thomas's eye, especially after the closet trick I pulled on Nick today. I take Joy with me as I step inside. The room is kind of dark.

"Nick?" I hear water running. I start down the hall. "Nick?"

"Yeah. I'm back here." I follow his voice. I step into the only room that's lit up and find him buttoning up his jeans. My voice comes out like a croak. "Where's your shirt? I mean…did you need something? Thomas sent me in here… but I'll just go wait out front."

His gaze drinks me in. "Maria…if you wanted to see me like this, all you had to do was ask." His voice is all sultry.

I tear my gaze from his chest and try to look him in the eye. "What! What are you talking about?"

He looks up at the ceiling. There's a slight chink in his confidence, and I think I see him blush. "Did you ask the girls…to take some…pictures…of just me?"

Now I'm embarrassed. I asked Abby to take a picture of him in his uniform. But I'm not admitting it now. I put my nose up in the air. "I did no such thing."

He's not ready to give up. I think his pride stings. He won't break his gaze, but I'm not looking away first. "If you say so."

I step up to him. "Do you really think I would ask high school girls to take pictures of you, and all of this, I point my finger up and down his body, for me?"

He smirks back at me. "I know you asked Abby to take pictures of me in my uniform. I heard you." He struts by me and bumps against me with his shoulder.

I'm so mad, I can't speak. I can't believe he heard me. "If you knew the answer, why'd you ask the question?" I ask his retreating back. He says nothing and just keeps on walking. "Do you need something, or can I go? It's going to be dark by the time we find a tree." I take Joy, shift her to my other hip, and march out.

Thomas leans on the side of his barrack wall. He hasn't moved since I went in.

"Did you find what you were looking for in there?"

I wheel around to face him. "No, Thomas. I did not. I was looking for a man, but instead I found a child."

Nick walks over to me. "Come on, Joy. Come to daddy." She leans straight over, and I almost drop her, but Nick is there to catch her.

"I'll be in the truck." I say to no one in particular.

Nick's hand goes for his pocket. "Here. You'll need these. It's locked."

I march away from all of them. I need some peace and quiet.

Chapter Nineteen

Just when I think I'll be sitting here all day, and it's getting cold, they all come walking out to the truck, including Thomas. What's he doing? He opens the truck door, and I hop out to let the girls climb in the back. I turn to put Joy back in the car seat between them. Nick crawls into the driver's seat and I sit by the door.

Thomas opens the door again. "Scoot over. I'm coming in."

"What? I don't think so."

"Scoot over, or I'm sitting on you." He shoves my leg with his hand.

I move over toward Nick, who I'm still irritated with. Thomas climbs up in the truck and shuts the door. He moves towards me until he's mashed up against the length of me. "Thomas. What are you doing?"

"I'm trying to get comfortable, but it's hard. You're going to have to move over more."

"Fine." I move clear away from him and now I'm mashed up against Nick. Thomas turns to me and flops his arms at his sides.

"Aw. That's better. I can breathe again. Okay, Nick. I've called ahead. We should be all clear to go out there. Hope you're all up for a bumpy ride." Eva and Abby stare at beautiful blonde Thomas in awe. They're all smiles.

"We're up for it." They high five each other over Joy's car seat, and she reaches up to touch their hands. It's the sweetest thing.

Nick fires up the truck. About two miles past the base, he turns off on a dirt road, and then another. Then he turns into a field. He takes us all down a dried mud path with deep, deep ruts. We bounce along. It feels like this truck's axle is going to break in half. Finally, the path smooths out again. He slows to a snail's pace.

"Alright, girls. Any tree out here is fair game. So pick a good one." Abby and Eva nod at Nick's instructions.

We get out and walk through a myriad of trees. I'm starting to think they all look the same. But then it happens.

Eva taps Nick's shoulder. "Stop! I found it." She stretches out her finger to point, and Abby does the same. In simultaneous slow motion, the girls point to the same tree.

I can't help but smile as they run to the tree, circle it, and take pictures. Nick reaches into the back of his truck and pulls out his chainsaw. Childhood memories catch me unaware. I recall walks in the woods with my dad. My eyes tear up before I can stop them.

I turn back to watch Nick march through the snow with the chainsaw at his side. I watch him start it up. Soon he's working away on the tree. It falls, and the chainsaw noise dies down. Nick, Thomas, and the girls carry the tree back to the truck, where Joy and I stand by, waiting. They manage to lift the tree into the back of the truck. The girls climb up in the back and drag the tree far enough back so Thomas can close the tailgate. Nick puts his chainsaw back in the box. I know I shouldn't, but I walk over to him. Joy remains on my hip. I grab him by the collar and pull him to me. I lean in and kiss him firmly on the lips. "Thanks for today."

Thomas steps up. "Hey, can I get in on that?"

I can't help but laugh. "Sure." I grab his collar and yank him down. I go for his lips but switch direction at the last minute and land a kiss on his cheek.

Thomas stands back up. "Ouch. Way to wound a guy's pride, Maria." He smiles over my head at Nick.

I carry Joy back to the truck. We go through the whole process of getting her back in her car seat again. I turn around to sit beside Nick. Thomas climbs in beside me, same as before. He splays his knees wide, and flops his arms down at his sides, taking up as much space as possible. He's such a brat, but I don't care. I don't mind having an excuse to scoot closer to Nick. I tingle all along the side of me as I rest up against him as we drive along the path, through the bumpiest of ruts. Finally, the worst of it is over, and we're back on the highway again.

He runs Thomas back to the barracks and gives him a parting salute.

We prepare for the long ride home. I decide to stay where I am, and he doesn't say anything. I lay my hand on his leg and give him a squeeze.

We're three hours down the road, and the cab is awfully quiet. I peek back at the girls, and they're all sleeping. I tap his leg. "Nick. Look in the back seat."

His eyes glance in the rearview mirror, and then they meet mine. He signals and pulls off the road.

"Nick, what are you doing?"

"What I wanted to do more of this morning." He pulls the rubber band from my hair and makes quick work of undoing my braid. His hands are in my hair, then back on my face. He brushes his thumbs across my lips. He leans in to kiss me with his hand still on my neck and in my hair. I grab his leg harder. I squeeze, then grip, as I try to keep myself grounded, but it's no use. I'm floating on air as his hands roam over all of me, and all I want is more. I give in for a while, reveling in the moment of this all-consuming desire; a feeling I've never experienced before. I didn't think Nick could make me burn any hotter than he has already, but I am wrong. Joy fusses from the back seat, and I snap out of it. I push on Nick's chest.

"Nick. You've got to stop. Joy's trying to wake, and we're still at least two hours from home. I think if you start the truck up again, she'll go back to sleep, but you've got to hurry up."

Nick gives a big sigh. "Alright."

Soon we're back on the road again. I scoot over to my window seat again and put distance between Nick and me.

"Have you got a pot at home?" What did he just say?

"Do I have pot?"

"No. Do you have a planting pot? Like, to hold the tree." He laughs and shakes his head.

Oh, yeah. The tree. Duh. "Yeah. I think I can find a pot big enough and heavy enough to hold it upright. I can't wait to see Joy's face this Christmas."

Nick coughs. "Yeah. It'll be pretty cute. She's really something."

I take a deep breath. "I guess we'll be decorating the house and everything." I hate that my voice is all flat and sad.

"What's the matter? Aren't you ready for Christmas?" Nick's voice is full of concern.

I feel bad. "I guess. Nick. I haven't really celebrated Christmas since I lost my baby. I was kind of getting through that, and then I lost my sister, and Christmas was Liz's favorite holiday." I sigh. "Liz was always festive enough for both of us. Being cheery and bright has never really been my thing."

He snorts. "You don't say."

I wipe a tear away. "So anyway, I just haven't been in the mood to celebrate much is all."

"Wasn't all this over a year ago?" His voice is whisper-quiet.

"Yeah. But it's just a hard time of year, you know? And every year, I wait to feel like Christmas cheer, but I haven't yet. And I figure, with me being alone, what's it matter if I celebrate or not? I keep thinking the feeling will come back, eventually, when I'm ready. And so I'm just waiting."

"That makes sense, I guess, but this year you have Joy. Do you want to decorate with me for Joy?" His voice is all hopeful.

I nod. My heart lifts a little at the thought of Joy in front of the Christmas tree. "Oh. Yeah, definitely. You know, for Joy."

"Yeah. For Joy." He reaches out, takes my hand in his, and pulls on it, until I give up and move over next to him again. He squeezes my hand as he moves it back to rest on his thigh. We ride on in silence. We're about forty-five minutes from home, and his hand goes slack in mine. I look over and he's nodding. I elbow him in the side.

"Nick! You can't fall asleep."

"Well then, talk to me." His words are slow and slurred.

"About what?"

"I don't know. Anything. Tell me…tell me about your first kiss."

No. I don't want to.

"Do I have to?"

He chuckles. "Yeah, you do. Make it as entertaining as possible, please."

I sigh. "I was old enough that when I was in grade school. We still played spin the bottle. You had to go in a dark closet, and kiss, or whatever. So, I'm at this party with a bunch of other seventh and eighth graders, and it's Halloween. But first, let me back up. See, I grew up in a ghost town. All the businesses had already been shut down by the time we lived there, and there were only fifty-two people living there, and that's counting people living five to ten miles out. My dad's job was twenty miles away. I guess he liked living where it was quiet. So anyway, the deal was, my classmate was having a dance at her house, but I had the haunted house at my place. So the kids would walk through our little shed, which we'd turned into a haunted house, and then they would walk the six to eight blocks to her house to the dance. My sister had helped me with the haunted house. She had made this creepy recording on a cassette tape to play when people walked through. My job was to be up in the rafters and hold a bucket of water to dump on the people as they walked by the doll hanging in the middle of the shed. It was great."

He shivers. "That sounds very creepy. But what about the kiss?"

"Oh, yeah. So, I dumped the water on different people, and this one kid, he freaked a little. He thought the doll threw up on him, and he ran out of that shed so fast! It was the best. Anyway. Afterwards, we all went to my neighbor's dance. About halfway through, a bunch of us went to sit at the base of a big tree in her yard, to play spin the bottle. So the bottle spins and it lands on me and the kid who thought the doll puked on him. He just happened to be my best friend's big brother, a guy all the girls liked. I didn't want to kiss him though because I had a boyfriend. But my boyfriend wasn't there that night because he didn't get to come to the party. I didn't want to go behind the big tree with my best friend's brother, but there was no getting out of it.

So, I went, and we just stood there for what felt like forever. But then, he bumped me up against the tree and leaned down to kiss me. I panicked. I turned my face sideways and raised my knee up at the same time, hitting him just right, and he fell to the ground, holding himself, moaning. It was super embarrassing. A bunch of kids ran around the tree. They weren't following the rules at all and they were all like 'What happened?' I didn't know what to say so I lied. I told them he kissed me, and so I kneed him in the nuts. And I guess he didn't want to lose his romantic reputation, because he didn't dispute my story. So, my first kiss was a farce, you might say."

"Hmmm. Well, where was your first real first kiss then?"

"At a dance in a barn." I smile at the memory. "He was the nicest boyfriend I ever had."

"How old were you?"

"I was thirteen. Where was your first kiss?" I'm kind of afraid to ask.

"Oh. My first kiss was when I was twelve. She was sixteen. She was my babysitter."

"You're kidding me. Please tell me you're kidding. Or I'll never hire another babysitter until Joy's like twenty. Well, no guys anyway."

He laughs. "Nope. I really was twelve, and she really was my babysitter. If it makes you feel any better, she was a very tiny sixteen-year-old who looked like she was thirteen, and I was a very tall twelve-year-old who looked like I was fourteen. I got my growth spurt early. I don't know. She was pretty. Who was I to say no?"

I punch him in the arm. "I get your point of view. But hers? That's just wrong. If you did anything else with her besides kissing, I don't want to know."

He laughs, and I'm scared to ask. "Yeah. Well. The first time she kissed me, we were watching E.T., and I got mad because she made me miss the ending, like the very last scene. It was so messed up. I made her rewind the VHS tape. Then, when my older brother got home later that night, they went in the other room for a while. She caused some pretty hard feelings between the two of us. But it didn't take me long for me to decide my relationship with my brother was definitely worth more than whatever I thought about the girl."

I squeeze his hand. "That's so messed up."

He sighs. "Yeah, well. I guess that's life in the hood."

I can't help but laugh. "There's a part of me that wants to go back to that time with you, and fight for your childhood. She messed with your emotions before you were ready for that."

He clears his throat. "Oh, we didn't do more than kiss. I

mean, I think she did the deed with one or two of my brothers, but not with me."

I don't know what to say to that, so I say nothing. I turn on the radio, and we search through the stations until we find soft rock. It isn't long and we're both singing to stay awake. Finally, we're back in our town. I ride with him as he drops Abby and Eva home. I wake them up, and they climb over the seat and kind of fall out the passenger door. "Thanks for today. Goodnight."

I call out after them. "Goodnight."

Nick starts to back out of their driveway. "Stop. Wait 'til they get inside please."

We drive home and I'm so ready for my bed, and that's when I remember I haven't washed the sheets yet since Joy got so sick. "Nick. Joy can't sleep in my bed. There may be a strawberry piece in it. She has to sleep with you."

"She's not sleeping with me unless you're there."

"She did last night."

"Yeah, she slept. But I didn't. I couldn't sleep with her snuggled all up against me all night when she's as hot as a furnace."

"Fine. We'll all sleep in one bed." I walked into that one, I know. I try not to worry when I remember I could take her to Daisy's room since she's gone, but I keep that thought to myself. I don't really want to sleep in Daisy's room, anyway. She wouldn't mind, but it just feels weird. We unload Joy together. I stagger into the house. I'm dead on my feet. I stumble into Nick's room, lay Joy down on the bed, and delayer her before changing her into a clean, dry diaper. I rush off to my room to change into sweats. I rush back to Nick's room and try not to panic as I see him lie down in his boxers and no shirt. "Aren't you going to get cold?"

"I always sleep like this." He looks all innocent, but I know better.

He lies down. I lay Joy next to him. She does what she

always does; shifts and wiggles until she's flush up against him. I sit on the edge of the bed. He gently moves her to the middle of his king-sized bed. It isn't long, and she's back where she was before he moved her away. He sighs. "Maria. I can't sleep with this little heater up against my side."

"Well, that's the side she sleeps on, and she likes to snuggle." I can't help but smile. She's so adorable. Her bright eyes go back and forth between our voices.

"Well, this is the side that I sleep on, and I don't like to snuggle." Nick frowns at me.

"What do you propose, then?" I think I know.

"You could always switch places with her. Then she can curl up next to you." He's all smug and happy.

"So I lay in the middle of you and Joy?" And get no sleep because you'll be laying right beside me with all your hotness. His grin is full wattage. I swear I go weak in the knees, and I'm sitting down! Darn the man. He thinks he's so smart. "Suit yourself."

I move Joy's little body closer to the edge as I move between her and Nick. Sure enough, soon, her hot little body is up against mine, but I don't care. I know I'll never get tired of her snuggling. I drift off to sleep and hold her to me to make sure she doesn't roll off the side of Nick's tall bed.

I wake in the middle of the night. Someone's hand grazes the side of my breast, and it isn't Joy's. I'm sandwiched between Joy and Nick. For all his talk about not sleeping all snuggly, I find it hard to believe right now. He spoons all along my backside. I take his offending hand and move it off me and down to his side. His arm pops right back up like it's spring loaded. This time he gets as far as my stomach, before I grab onto him and lace my fingers through his, to keep him from drifting any farther north. It takes me forever, but I finally get back to sleep.

The next time I wake, it's morning. I feel a nuzzling on the back of my neck. His big foot wedges between mine under the covers, and his leg gooses me as I lay here. Joy sleeps. Her beautiful dark curls head all different directions.

"Nick. What are you doing?"

I hear his low, sexy laugh. "What comes naturally."

"Well, stop." I sit up and brush his hand off me for about the tenth time.

He reaches for me. "Where are you going?"

"Breakfast doesn't make itself. You can lay here with Joy, I'll get it. There's no need for us to both be here."

He sighs and flips off the covers. He rolls off the bed and stretches as he wakes.

Nick is too gorgeous for his own good. I want to look away, but I just keep staring at his chest.

He growls at me. "You keep lookin' at me like that, woman, and I'm climbin' right back in."

My face is on fire. I turn away from him and curl up next to Joy. I peek back at him as he throws on a shirt and a pair of shorts.

He sighs. "I guess I'll go cook up some breakfast. But after that, I've got to get to work on that pamphlet for the Christmas jars event."

"Okay. I think Joy and I will just kind of hang out here this morning. She's had a long couple of days." I've had a few long days too. I need to chill out.

He leaves the room and I run down the hall to my diary, which I've been neglecting.

Dear Diary,

Things are not any clearer than they were a few days ago. I don't know what I'm going to do. I want a permanent solution for Joy, and I want it now. I hate that her future is so uncertain. I only want to take care of her, but Nick is the only person who has legal rights to her. I know it's not fair for me to assume he won't stick around, but it's such a big commitment! It's a lot to ask of him.

The problem is that I can't let Joy go, but I don't know if I will always be in Nick's life. I don't want to guilt him into marrying me, and I don't want him to feel obligated, either. We can't live together as friends for very long either. There's too much attraction between us. Too many times I've come so close to giving in. I know it would be wonderful to be with Nick. I have no doubts about that. But if we're together, it will cloud my judgment, and I can't risk Joy's future.

-Maria

Chapter Twenty

I head to the kitchen for coffee while I wait for Joy to wake up. Nick's in his usual position; standing at the stove with a hot skillet. My body betrays me. The mere sight of him makes my mouth water. He may as well be frying my eggs.

I feel the need to announce myself. "I heard the coffee pot beep. Joy's sleeping. I thought I'd just grab a cup."

"Knock yourself out." He winks at me.

"Thank you. What are you making this morning?" I feel weird being all polite, but I don't know what to do.

"I'm heating oil. I'm going to make pancakes." He studies me like he's waiting for me to say something. What does he want to hear?

"Yum. I'll just grab an apple or something. I'm trying to cut down on carbs."

He looks me up and down. "Why?"

I feel self-conscious. Why can't I keep my mouth shut. "I'm trying to lose a little weight. I have been for about a year now. It's not going so well. It probably doesn't help that I work long hours, eat at irregular times, and don't get enough sleep. You know."

"You look fine to me." He raises his coffee cup to his lips

and peers over at me as he sips it. He sets it back down and removes the hot skillet from the heat. He flips off the burner. He towers over me. His hands rest on my hips. He tugs me towards him. "But, if you feel like exercising I know the perfect thing."

I sigh and lean backwards against the counter and away from him. "Nick. Seriously. Do you ever stop?"

He leans. His hands find the counter on both sides. He's boxing me in. It's incredibly hot. "Not unless I'm told, and that never happens; if you know what I mean."

Why is this naughtiness so much fun? "Good one, Nick. You're just full of one-liners. Think you're so clever…"

His eyes burn like fire. He lifts me off the floor and jars me as he drops me on the counter. I barely manage to regain my balance. He stands right in front of me and wedges himself between my knees. His hands grip my hips.

"Damn it, Maria. I'm dying over here. I don't feel clever, I feel anything but! I've been waiting for you to see me, to notice me. I've tried keeping my distance, but I can't stay away. Your eyes follow me everywhere. They're always on me. I know you want me." He leaves a trail of kisses on my neck and down my collarbone. Any more of this and I'm going to go up in flames.

"Nick." I nudge him away. "We've had this conversation too many times. It's too fast. I can't just do what I feel like doing. I've got to think of Joy!"

His grip on my hips tightens. It's almost painful. "You're just using her as someone to hide behind. You're scared of getting hurt. You're scared of a relationship. You're scared of me. But it could be so good, Maria. You and I could be so good together."

I know that, but I ignore it.

"You think I have any doubts about you in the bedroom? I don't. But I need answers, Nick. I can't just be with you because it'd be nice, because we both want it. I need more than that." I'm so muddled, I don't even know what I'm asking for.

His eyes implore me. "Then tell me what you need."

I'm so frustrated. "I want to know what's in Joy's future. I want to know where I fit in. I want to know where you fit in."

He looks at me like I'm a simpleton. "I'm her father. That's where I fit in."

"Okay, fine. How long are you planning on living here? Where do you want to end up? Where is Joy going to go to school? What are your career plans?"

Nick slaps the counter for emphasis. "I don't have definite answers to all those questions, Maria. I've been accommodating your schedule, trying to help you with Joy. I thought that's what you wanted. I thought that's what you needed." He steps back. "You never told me you wanted me to figure things out. If you want a plan for Joy, I'll give you a plan."

Now I'm irritated. "I have a plan, Nick. Daisy and Dale will watch Joy when I'm at work, and when she gets old enough, between the three of us, one of us can take her to school and another can pick her up. I'm sure it'll be fine."

Nick sighs heavily. He looks at the floor, shakes his head, and pinches the bridge of his nose. His head snaps back up, and he looks me in the eye. "So basically, you made plans for Joy's whole life without me, even though I'm her father, and the only blood relative she's got, that you know of." Nick's whole manner changes and his eyes are as cold as ice. "If you don't need me here, if you've got everything under control, I'll go. But when I come back, I'll bring my lawyer, and we can sort everything out that way. Is that you want?"

I hop down off the counter and reach out to him.

"Don't…touch…me…" His words are biting, and they rip me in two.

"Nick, I was only trying to be prepared. I needed a backup plan. For Joy." I try to reason with him, but it's no use. I see that now, but it's a little too late.

He puts up his hands as if to silence me. "You're still doing it. You're still using Joy as a shield to hide behind. You don't need a backup plan for Joy. You need a backup plan for you. You're so bent on not getting hurt, I never had a chance with you. It was over for us before it even started. I'm done."

He marches back to his room. Minutes later, he's back in the kitchen. I'm still standing where he left me. His bag hits the floor. I back away instinctively as he comes at me until I'm cornered. He glares down at me, and I glare right back.

"So you're just going to leave, just like that?"

"Why would I stay?" His eyes are full of pain. "You don't want me here. You don't need me here."

I'm on the verge of crying, even though I know I'm completely at fault. "What about Joy?"

"Make no mistake, Maria. I'll be back for her. You'll still see her, but it'll be on my terms." His words chill me to the bone.

"Nick! How could you do this to me? I need her. And she needs me." I call after him as he walks away.

He turns back and rushes me. "Maria." He takes my face in his hands and brushes his lips on mine, back and forth, asking permission, and then he plunges, breaking down my defenses. He doesn't stop until I'm all wrapped up in him, forgetting myself completely. He backs away. Anger and frustration are written all over his face. "*I* need you, but you're too afraid to jump. Leaving is all I've got left."

Chapter Twenty-One

Fortunately for me, Joy doesn't mind spending the whole day in bed, or a weepy pouty-faced me who brought all my troubles on myself, but still I wallow. I lay here, playing patty cake games with Joy; mindlessly watching Sheriff Longmire on Netflix in the background. I mostly hide my crying spells so I don't scare or upset her. I keep checking my phone, even though I know it's no use. Nick's not going to call me, or text me, or send me silly Snapchats. Not anymore. I've ruined everything that was between us, and my worst fears are coming true. He's going to take Joy.

The day's almost over. I hear a vehicle outside. Maybe he came back! I rush to the front door. It's Dale and Daisy. Oh no. How am I going to tell them what happened? Daisy comes in with Dale on her heels. "Where's my little Joy? I need some about right now."

Oh, dear. "Why? What's wrong?"

"Oh, nothing really. Dale and I just had a disagreement. It lasted the last twelve hours or so. That's all."

Dale stomps back to his room and doesn't say a word.

I hand Joy over to Daisy. I try to keep it together, but the dam breaks all over again. I bawl my eyes out.

Daisy waits about ten seconds, and then she gives a big sigh. "Maria. Get a hold of yourself. You sound like a dying heifer." Her scolding snaps me out of my crying jag.

"I can't believe you just called me a heifer! Why would you do that?" I forgot how mean Daisy can be.

"It made you stop crying, didn't it? Now, I'm guessing this has something to do with the fact that a big black truck is no longer parked in my driveway."

I nod my head. Fat tears start rolling down my cheeks.

Daisy carries Joy to the highchair and puts her in it. She gets to work chopping up bananas, Joy's favorite. Seeing the bananas reminds me of the strawberries. "Don't give her strawberries. Ever. She's deathly allergic."

Daisy looks intently at me. "You should never give a baby strawberries, Maria. I thought you knew that. You're a nurse."

I roll my eyes. "It was an accident."

Daisy shakes her head. "I'm guessing you've got a lot to tell me. Sit yourself down. I'll make you some chamomile tea."

I sit down at the table. Before I know it, I'm telling Daisy everything that's happened over the past few days, except for all the heated kisses and Nick's chasing me nonstop. Daisy brings the tea over and sits down at the table. That's when I tell her about Nick's ultimatum, and that he said he's coming back for Joy.

"Oh, Daisy. I don't know what I'm going to do. I don't think I can bear to lose Joy, but I don't think I have much choice."

"Maria. There's always a choice. It may be unconventional, and maybe not what be what you anticipated, but you could follow Nick and Joy. You're a nurse, and you're unattached. You could go anywhere! The opportunities are endless. There will always be another nursing job, but there's not another Joy."

"Or Nick." I mutter under my breath.

"What was that?" By the look on her face, I think she heard me, but Daisy can be ornery.

"Nothing. I just, I just can't believe he said those things. I can't believe he just up and left."

"Did you do anything to lead him on?" Daisy stares at me.

"No. I never had a chance to! I mean, he was forever chasing after me, getting in my space. He knows he's my weakness. He knows he's hard to resist. You've seen him. What girl could resist all that?" I fiddle with a rubber band. "Maybe I led him on a few times, but he started it."

Daisy's eyes search my face. "Are you afraid he'll be unfaithful?"

"No. It's not that. I just. He's so intense, you know? And he's so…physical." I blush. I sound like a nun.

Daisy goes still. "Did he hit you? Or threaten you?!"

"No. I just mean he has a very physical presence. He's very manly." I glance at her. She's amused.

She giggles. "And this is a bad thing?"

"I don't know. It's hard to explain. He's just…he's just so intimidating."

Dale clears his throat and walks from the living room to the kitchen. "I tried to tell him."

"What'd you tell him, Dale?" I'm afraid to ask.

"I told Nick to drop the full-court press. I know you, Maria. I knew his aggression would scare you off."

This is so embarrassing, but I feel a little better. If Nick's behavior was bad enough that Dale noticed, then I know I'm not exaggerating.

I feel foolish having this discussion with an old married couple, but I've got no one else. "I thought I could ignore all his advances. But he was relentless. And I wasn't sure where he thought it was going. I mean, I couldn't tell if he was after a conquest, or something lasting."

Daisy taps my hand. "What are you saying, Maria? What if

he was looking for a commitment from you? Would you give him one?"

My heart skips a beat at the thought of being married to Nick. "I don't know."

Her face morphs into mom-mode. "You know I always speak my mind."

"Yes, Daisy. I know."

"It's better for Joy if she has two parents. I'm sure you could give her all the love you have, and it would be enough, if it had to be. And I know her mother left Joy with you. But the fact doesn't change that Nick's most likely her father, and he wants to be in her life. I haven't known him a long time, but I can see he's a good man. You can take him at his word."

"Daisy." I'm exasperated. "Nick's also a charmer. You've only just met him."

"This is true, but I think I'm a pretty good judge of character. I didn't know you long before you moved in, and I was right about you. You can't hold his looks and his charisma against him. It isn't fair. I think you need to take a step back and re-evaluate everything. Don't think about Nick's looks. Think about everything he's done since you met him, every decision he's made. Then reconsider if what you're doing is best for Joy, or if it's best for you."

Dear Diary –

I hate it when Daisy's right. That's all I'm saying today.

- Maria

Chapter Twenty-Two

I check my phone calendar twice. Today's Christmas tree decorating day down at the L. J. Youth Center. I remember what Nick said about showing volunteerism; I pack up Joy and her Johnny Jumper and we head down there.

Christmas music plays. There are cookies out on the table. The tree is halfway done. Eva and Abby look surprised to see me. "Oh. Hey, Maria."

I step closer and recognize the tree in the big planter. "Isn't that the tree Nick cut down?" Speak of the devil and he appears. I can't believe how much I miss him. "Nick? What are you doing here?"

"Eva texted me. It's decorating the tree day, and I didn't want to miss it. I thought we may as well put the tree to use down here. Plus, I didn't want to drag it into Daisy's house and make a mess on the carpet. It'll be easy to sweep up this cement floor." He sounds all nervous.

I've never seen him this way.

"Well. Since you're here, would you mind hanging up Joy's jumper in the doorway? I can't reach it without a ladder." I hate to ask him, but he does it so well.

"Sure."

"Um, okay. I'll just go get it from the car." I feel lost.

Abby walks over. "Maria. I can take Joy."

"Oh. Thank you."

Nick's already walking to my car. I run to catch up to him as I call out, "Do you want me to go home?"

He wheels around to face me. "Why would I want that?"

"Forget it. Did you drive in this morning?" I have no right to ask him these questions.

"No. I've been staying in a hotel. The price isn't too bad, and they have free continental breakfast, so that's nice. Keys?"

I hand them to him, our hands touch. The familiar zing is there, but he doesn't react. He grabs the jumper from my car, and we head back to the youth center, not talking.

"So you'll let me know when to be here for the community event? I don't want to be late. I'll bring Thomas. He loves to bake, and he loves an audience."

I nod my head like a puppet. "Thanks, Nick. I really appreciate it."

"Sure, Maria. Happy to help." His polite, agreeable voice wounds me.

He walks on ahead of me and doesn't look back. I tell myself this is what I wanted. I join in the decorating with the kids, and soon my sadness leaves. I hum Christmas carols and get caught up in the kids happy chattering and laughter as they decorate the tree. We barely finish, and a delivery guy pulls up, dropping off a bunch of sandwiches from the local sandwich shop. Nick rushes over with his wallet. "I've got it. What's the damage?"

The teenagers and the adults all sit down at the table. Nick runs over to grab Joy. He sits at the head of the table, and I can't help but laugh as he takes a big bite of sandwich and Joy's eyes follow the sandwich all the way to his mouth. She reaches out to grab it. He sets it down, far away from her. I jump up, grab a piece of bread and some cheese and crumble them up into swallow-sized pieces on a plate. I put it down in front of her. I run to the kitchen to fill her sippy cup with some juice diluted with water and hand it to Nick.

"Thanks, Maria."

I sit down to eat my sandwich, and I can't help but notice Nick at the end of the table. He holds little Joy, enjoys his sandwich, and carries on with everyone here. He looks right at home. He's so at ease with everyone. Is what Daisy said true? Do I feel threatened by him? Am I really willing to spend the rest of my life alone to avoid the risk of being hurt? I snap out of my reverie as everyone gets up to throw their plates away.

Eva claps her hands. "Now that the table is clear, and the food is put away, it's time to make a paper chain."

"Yep." Abby nods her head. "But our paper chain is going to be different. We need everyone's help to make it. What you do is write three wishes on three different pieces of paper, then roll the paper so the wishes are on the inside. And the wishes can be personal, like a healing prayer for someone you know; or a more general wish for everyone like world peace, or less pollution, whatever." She looks over at Eva.

"Yeah. And then we make one big chain of all these wishes, with some blank pieces in between, and hang it around the tree so if anyone comes in and wants to add their wishes at any time, they can. And, when Christmas is over, we take the chain of wishes and we put them all in a big jar and put the lid on it and save it." The room gets quiet as everyone gets to work writing down their wishes. We stand in line and wait to staple our papers to add to the chain. What I wrote doesn't make sense to me, but I wrote it anyway. That's what wishes are; dreams that we hope for, even if they seem out of reach.

The afternoon passes quickly, and I feel filled with Christmas cheer by the time the day's over. I pack up Joy's playpen and wrestle it into my trunk. I go back for the jumper that's still hanging in the doorframe. I look around, but I don't see Nick anywhere. I go to the back and grab the step ladder. I unfold it and set it down. I shake it to make sure it doesn't move. I climb up the steps and try to keep my knees from shaking. Heights make me nervous. The jumper's stuck tight to the doorframe. I finally figure out the mechanism and get the one side loose. I tug on the other side, and it finally gives, as it drops to the floor. Relieved, I start back down the ladder, but someone bumps it, and I start to fall backwards.

I land in someone's arms. I know it's Nick from his feel and smell. It's a domino effect in slow motion. I land on Nick, and he starts to fall backwards, but then someone catches him. It's big Gary, who works on the dock in the warehouse. "Easy there, Nick."

"Thanks, Gary. I can't believe I almost fell."

I find my voice. "Nick. I'm fine now. You can put me down."

"Thank goodness for Gary." Nick's still looking at me. "My feet got all tangled up in the wire. That's why I almost fell. I saw the ladder move, and I ran to catch you. In my hurry, I didn't see the wire piled up on the floor."

"Thank God I came out here to pick up my wire." Gary runs his hands through his hair. "I'm sorry guys."

"No harm, no foul." Nick pats him on the shoulder.

Roman walks by rubbing his shoulder and griping to his friend, Rafael. "Stupid ladder. I ran into it walking backwards when I was carrying those 2x4s. Who leaves a ladder in a doorway?"

I can't help it. I bust out laughing, and pretty soon the men are too.

Roman looks back, gives us a funny look, and then continues on his way.

Nick walks me out to the car. He carries Joy while I carry the jumper. I turn to him and take Joy into my arms. "That could have been a bad deal."

He gives me a sad smile. "It's a good reminder."

"What do you mean?"

"Sometimes we all get so focused on what we're doing, that

we can't see it might be hurting someone else." He sighs. "I'm sorry about the words I said the last time we spoke. I want what's best for Joy, too. I'm still thinking about all of this, what the best answer is for her. I'd like to be your friend. We should be able to figure this out without any lawyers."

"Thanks, Nick." My heart sinks at the word friend. "That means a lot to me. I've been doing some thinking myself, reevaluating recent life changes, and the choices I need to make. Yes, I'd love to be friends."

Dear Diary,

I got what I asked for. Nick has decided to forgive me, and we are now friends. If this is what I wanted, why do I find myself missing the man who pushed every boundary I set and crossed every line? This new Nick is reserved and polite, and I hate it.

-Maria

Chapter Twenty-Three

The next three days pass by quickly at work, and I'm glad for the distraction. I'm surprised to find myself looking at the stove and missing Nick's presence as I get ready in the morning. I go to grab my coffee cup from the cupboard. I long for his looming presence, hovering over me, and getting in my space. This is all so confusing.

By the third day of work, I come home, bone tired. I plop down at the dinner table, and that's when I notice how quiet the house is. There's a casserole on the stove, and the table is set for two, complete with candles and a flower-filled vase. This has Daisy written all over it. There's a note.

> Dear Maria.
>
> We thought you'd like a dinner guest. Everything is ready. Please change out of your scrubs. – Daisy
>
> P.S. If this goes South, this was Daisy's idea, not mine. - Dale.

I race back to the bedroom. I'm all excited. Since I'm dining in, and not going out in the cold, I decide to wear a dress. I don't think Nick's ever seen me in one. I choose a yellow plaid one; it was my sister's favorite on me. She had great fashion taste, so I trust her judgment.

I spray on a little perfume and dab on a bit of lip gloss. The doorbell rings and I slip on my sandals to answer the front door.

"Richard?"

"Hey. I, uh. I got your text." He holds flowers out to me.

I'm thoroughly confused, but I hear Daisy's voice inside my head, chiding me. "Always be hospitable." I reach out and take the bouquet. "They're lovely. Thank you. Please come in."

"Thanks." His tall frame fills the doorway. I feel strange having Richard in my home. "Mmm. Something smells good! Beats my cookin' anyways."

"Please." I stumble around and try to get my bearings. "Have a seat at the table. I'll be…right back. I just, uh. I forgot something."

I race back down the hallway and grab my phone off my dresser. I scan my texts.

Richard. This may seem out of the blue, but would you like to have dinner with me tonight? I did not send this! I'm going to give Daisy a piece of my mind when I see her next. That scheming matchmaker! I can't believe she got into my phone!

The front door shuts. "Maria?" I'd recognize that voice anywhere. Crap. What's Nick doing here? I'm going to kill Daisy.

I race back up the hallway. "Heyyy, Nick. I was just having supper with Richard. Would you like to join us?"

Uncertainty is written all over his face. "I rushed right over. Daisy said you needed my help?"

I step closer to him, whispering. "I think Daisy called up more than one man tonight." I motion with my head to the kitchen. "She called Richard over here for supper. With me. Alone."

Nick gives me an ornery smile, and I see a shade of the old Nick I used to know. "Well. Thanks for the dinner invite, but I already got take-out. I think I'll just head over to the hotel. Looks like you've got things under control here." He steps toward the kitchen and peeks in. "Bye, Richard. Have a nice night."

I glare at his back as he walks out the door.

"Maria?" Richard calls to me.

I'm being a terrible hostess. I walk back in the kitchen. "I'm so sorry to keep you waiting, Richard. Nick's visit was unexpected."

"Oh? You two seem kind of close, but you don't talk about him at work." Richard looks confused. He has every right to be. I'm so going to give Daisy a piece of my mind.

"Yes. Well, it's kind of complicated."

"What's that mean?"

I laugh nervously. "It means I sort of inherited a beautiful baby girl named Joy. She literally showed up on my doorstep. And Nick just happens to be her father. But, in my defense, I met Joy first. And in his defense, he didn't know she existed until about two weeks ago. So. That's my life now."

Richard's face is almost comical. I can see he's trying to find the right words to say. I reach out and take his hand. "Relax, Richard. I'm not looking for a husband, or rather someone to help me keep Joy. Nick and I…well, we'll just have to figure out our dynamics for the sake of Joy. I want to continue being a big part of her life, and so does he, of course, because he's her father." I raise my hand. "But Joy's mom left me a letter and asked me to watch over her daughter, so you see why I have to be here for Joy." I lean back in my chair. "And Nick just found out he was a dad. As I said already. So, it's um. Well, it's complicated."

Richard is silent. He studies my face. "Why don't you two just get married? Wouldn't that be the easiest choice?"

"I don't think that's an option." I let out a breath. "You know what? I'm monopolizing tonight with my problems. Let's talk about something else."

"Well." Richard laughs and leans back in his chair. "Now that we've established that you and I are not going to happen, do you know any single women looking for a good time with a good guy?"

I grab his arm and give a small squeeze. "Richard! As a matter of fact, I might." I whip out my phone, and he leans in. Richard stays longer than I thought he would, and we have a very nice time together. He's a pretty great guy and we have the same sense of humor, as I found out while we were scrolling through all my Facebook friends. I manage to find a few women he agreed to go on a blind date with. I pause and look in his eyes. "You know what? This has been the best time I've had in quite a while. I don't think I've ever had a guy friend who wasn't interested in something else." I smile to myself. "It's an argument I had with Nick."

"Maria." Richard clears his throat. "I have to agree with Nick on that account. Women and men cannot stay friends very easily. It just doesn't work. Because the majority of men will always think of a woman in a sexual way, and if they're both single, you can bet the man is not going to be friends with a woman he doesn't consider sexually attractive on some level. It is what it is."

I smack his arm. "I don't believe you."

He laughs. "Agree to disagree, then."

I laugh. "And on that note: would you like to go to the late movie with me? I haven't been in so long, and I'm still upset with Daisy for inviting you to dinner and not telling me. On top of that, she called Nick with a fake emergency! She was trying to cause a scene tonight."

Richard smiles down at me. "So you want to go to a movie with me to make Daisy think tonight is going how she wants it to?"

"No. I want to go to the movie tonight so that she has to stay up late waiting for me to return home. And when I do get back here, I'm going to tell her that you decided I have too much baggage, and that's why it didn't work. You see, I've been having a running argument with her. She says if I meet the right guy, it won't matter that I already have a baby but I disagree."

Richard clears his throat again. "I'll go to the movie with you because we're getting on so well, and I haven't been to a movie in ages. But I agree with Daisy. If the right man comes along, it wouldn't matter if you had four children. If he loves you, he'll love your children too. It's that simple. And, I might want to add, I'm not that guy. At least not for you."

"Thanks for your honesty, Richard. What movie are we going to see?"

It's almost midnight when Richard drives me home. I get out of the car to go in. He hops out, too. "Maria."

"Yeah?" He walks me to the front door.

"I'd like to kiss you. Just once. I've always wondered…"

"Considering you went along with everything so willingly tonight, despite the fact that you were tricked by my meddling, elderly roommate, sure."

Richard takes my hand in his and leans down. He gives me a soft kiss on the lips. It's nice, but it's nothing compared to Nick. I open my eyes and look up at him. He looks disappointed or amused, I can't tell. "I guess I'll never have to wonder now."

Should I be insulted? "Was I that bad?"

"It was…well it was like if I kissed my cousin?"

"Gross! It didn't feel *incestuous* to me, but there was no spark." Not that I would know since I've never kissed a family member.

"Yeah. That's it. I didn't feel any spark either. Goodnight, Maria. See you at work."

Daisy throws open the door, and it almost hits me! "Maria."

"Daisy." I walk by her and go down the hallway to my room. I think I'll let her wonder for a while longer. Joy's fast asleep on my bed. She's so precious. And she's growing so fast! I fall asleep thinking about Richard's question about marriage and Nick. I can't help but think it would be a wonderful adventure.

Chapter Twenty-Four

Daisy's at the table with Joy by the time I get up. I throw on a hoodie and my sleep pants and wander to the coffeepot. I grab a cup. I stop by the fridge for the milk. I plop down in a chair with my banana. Joy holds out her hand to me. "Nana?" Those are the sweetest words I've ever heard. My baby is a genius!

I feel like dancing. "Daisy, did you hear that? She said nana!" I rush over to Joy. "Of course, you can have some nana, sweetheart. Here's more nana."

Daisy frowns at me. "I think she was calling me nana because that's what I am. I'm her grandma." She winks at Joy. "Ain't that right, sugarplum? I'm your nana." Daisy watches me. "How was your dinner date last night?"

"It was great." I smile and try to look all dreamy. "Richard's a super nice guy. I mean just the best. We have the same sense of humor. He's a great listener. We left the house for a while and went to the movies."

Daisy's watching me like a hawk. "And how was your goodnight kiss?"

"I beg your pardon. Were you spying on me through the

kitchen window?" I knew she was, but I didn't think she'd admit to it.

"I was merely waiting for you to get home. You know how I worry. And I just happened to see the kiss."

Nick's head pops around the corner.

I didn't even know he was in the house. "Nick?" How much did he hear? By the look on his face, I'd say all of it.

"Hey, Maria. Daisy, I fixed your sink. I'll head back over to the hotel. Call me if you need anything else." His voice is flat and emotionless.

"Nick." I chase him out to his truck and stand near his door. "I was just messing with Daisy. It was just one kiss. It didn't mean anything."

He gives me a forced grin. "What do I care?"

Sucker punch, and I'm down for the count. "I guess I deserved that."

Nick's not done. "What about Richard? What does he deserve?"

I'm not following. "What do you mean?"

"Are you for real right now? Are you going to string him along just like you did me, or did you tell him you can only be friends, because you can't handle any *emotion*. I thought you were a nice person, Maria. A real person. But you're not. You're just like all those other women. You play games with people's lives and mess with their heads. I don't need that, and neither does Richard. We both deserve better." His fists clench at his sides. "You're done playing with me."

I catch my breath. "Richard knows, Nick. He knows Daisy texted him, not me. He knows that we're only meant to be friends. And he's okay with that. My life right now, it's too complicated for him. *He* said that. Not me. We even went through my Facebook friends to try to find him a blind date. We're just friends."

Nick looks at me like he wants to believe me, and this gives me hope. "If you're just friends, what was the kiss about?"

"Oh. Well, he walked me to my door, and he asked if he could kiss me. He…he said he didn't want to always wonder what it would be like." I look down at the ground.

"So what I said about guys always wanting to be more than friends with girls is true then?" I hate the satisfaction in Nick's voice.

"I suppose you could say that, yes. Richard and I are still friends, and he's really funny! But he's definitely interested in only friendship. So, see, it's possible." I stick out my tongue like a child.

Nick's eyes narrow. "Agree to disagree. What about the kiss? Did it mean anything to you?"

The guy must be deaf. "I just told you it didn't. Why are you asking me again?"

"Did you…did you feel anything?"

Stop beating a dead horse, Nick. It's not your business, anyway.

"I just told you! We're just friends, We both agreed."

"That's not what I asked. I want to know how you felt when he kissed you!"

Why?

"Well, I don't have to tell you that!" I cross my arms. I hate the smug look on his face right now, and I almost lie to him, but I can't.

"You're not telling me, because there was no spark."

"Listen up and listen close, Nick Laus." I hold up my finger. "One. You don't even know what you're talking about. And two, if there was no spark, that's because he was a gentleman, and he didn't maul me…like some people I know."

Nick slaps his truck and points a finger at me. "You just admitted there was no spark and that you like the way I kiss you."

I throw my hands up. "That's not what I said at all. I'm going back inside. I came out here to tell you Richard and I are friends, and that I have nothing to hide. I've done that. So goodbye."

He's still smiling. "I'll see you in a few days, Maria. Don't forget the community baking event."

"Okay. I'll see you later. I'm going to go stroller shopping for Joy today. I can't believe I didn't do this sooner. I want to get like one of those jogging strollers? And I'm thinking about trading in my Honda Fit for something bigger."

Nick snorts behind me. "Anything's bigger than an oversized, enclosed motorized pushcart attached to a bicycle, and that's basically what your Chloe is."

I walk back inside, but I can't stop grinning at Nick's exaggerated description of Chloe. I think I'm growing on him.

"Maria?" Nick calls out. "Let me go with you. Please. I'd like to. I mean, I'd like to be a part of choosing the stroller Joy's going to ride in, and I think I could be helpful in choosing the right car for you and Joy."

It's only right since Joy is his daughter. I wheel back around. "You know I'm perfectly capable of doing these things on my own. But since you asked so nice, okay. How about you come back at noon, and then the three of us can go on a little shopping trip?"

Nick gives me a little smile. "Sounds good. I'll see you then."

Daisy's still at the table when I return to the kitchen. "How'd Nick take the news?

"What news?" I know exactly what she's talking about but baiting her is too much fun. Besides, she deserves a lot of heck after the prank she pulled.

"The news that you kissed Richard?"

I answer all casual. "He was fine with it. He doesn't care. Nick told me we're just friends now."

Daisy wrings her hands together. "That's all he said?"

I'm not going easy on her. "What did you think he would say? Did you perhaps send him a text message…from me…or call him telling him to come over here?" I stare her down. She doesn't flinch.

"So, I meddled in your love life, Maria, but it needed to be done. You certainly weren't going to take any action! All you seem capable of is chasing men away. That's no way to live your life."

"Daisy. I know you think you're doing good, but you need to stop. Fortunately for you, Richard's a gentleman. He didn't even get mad at you when I told him you'd texted him and not me. And it turns out we have a lot in common, and we've decided to be friends. He doesn't want more than that from me, given I'm pretty attached to Joy now."

"So." Daisy sits back and smiles at me. She's all confidence. "Because of my text to Richard, you both gained a friend, and he'll never worry that you were the one who got away, because you kissed, and it just wasn't there. What's so bad about any of that?"

Nothing. Nothing at all. She's maddening.

Dale stands in the corner, chuckling. "You can try, Maria. But you won't win. Daisy's pretty hard-headed when she sets her mind on something. Right now, she's set on finding you a husband."

Daisy shakes her finger at me. "Say what you will, both of you. But where there's a will there's a way. And there's the power of prayer. I've been praying for a husband for Maria since the day I met her." She takes my hand. "Maria. I've been praying for your happiness too. God listens. I believe your happiness is already here." She nods her head in Joy's direction. "You just have to be willing to accept it."

I take back my hand, shaken by Daisy's words. I wish I could feel half as sure as her about my future love life and Joy. "I'm going to take a shower now. Nick's coming back around noon. He's going to go stroller shopping with me. And then, we might look at cars. My Honda's kind of small to be hauling Joy around in. I'd like something bigger."

"That's a fine idea." Daisy's eyes light up. "Did you ever fill out that job application for the school nurse job?"

"Um. No. I've been thinking about that some more, and I kind of like working three days on, four days off. I still get home most days by six or seven, and for now, that works. The main thing is I get to work days, and I waited so long to come off nights, I don't want to lose my shift."

❄

Nick shows back up in the truck, and we decide to take it stroller shopping, as we're not sure if a jogger stroller will fit in my little trunk. Joy's whole face lights up when she sees Nick. "Da da."

"Hey pumpkin. How's my girl?" We get her situated in the back of the king cab in her car seat. "I've done some online looking since this morning, and I've narrowed it down to one store, but it's the next town over. Is that alright?"

"Yeah. Sure. I mean, if you don't mind. I'm up for a drive."

"Alright. Cool." We get to the store, and it doesn't take long to agree on the stroller. He loads it up. The next place we stop is a park.

"Nick. What are we doing here?"

"I thought it'd be nice to test out the stroller." He unloads it from the back of the truck. I get Joy out of her car seat and he comes around to get her. He puts her in the stroller, and I check her coat and hat. We walk the sidewalk that goes around the lake at the park.

Nick stops for a second. He looks at me with a serious expression on his face. We start walking again, and he starts talking. "When I was growing up, I never thought I'd live past the age of twenty-five. For a long time, I thought I'd die in the same neighborhood my brothers did. There was so much violence, and I couldn't see a way out. The day the ROTC recruiter showed up at my high school, I saw my chance. I grabbed on with both hands. My friends made fun of me. Most of them stopped hanging out with me, but I didn't care.

I had somewhere to go on the weekends. I had a means to leave town, to escape. Most of my friends, my classmates, they were partying and a lot of them became young parents. It's not that I thought was better than them, but I knew that life wasn't for me. I wasn't going to do anything to mess up my future, or anything that would tie me down and keep me from getting out of my neighborhood. I kept that rule even after I joined the army. I didn't mess around with women. Where I grew up, and the things I saw, they stayed with me. I didn't want to live so recklessly. I may have made a mistake with Joy's mother. But that was one mistake, Maria. And I'm going to do right by Joy. I'm going to be in her life and take care of her, as long as I'm able. I just want you to know that I'm not going anywhere."

I touch Nick's hand. "Thank you for sharing that with me. I'm glad to hear your intentions, Nick. Joy deserves that from you. And I believe you. I'm sorry I ever doubted your intentions as a father."

We walk for about an hour. I never tire of watching Joy's little feet kick happily, as she points her finger at things she sees. Her eyes light up and she gets all excited. We return to the truck, and I help her out of the stroller. She starts fussing and pointing at the stroller. Nick starts laughing. "I think she likes her stroller."

He folds it up and puts it in the back of the truck. We head back to the house to switch vehicles. By the time we get home, Joy's sound asleep. I take the whole car seat inside to Daisy. "I'm just going to use the bathroom, and then the three of us are going car shopping."

Daisy chuckles and gazes down at sleeping baby Joy. "Why don't you and Nick go car shopping and leave Joy with me? It'll be a lot easier."

"Thanks, Daisy." I smile. "I hate to wake her."

Nick stands by my car. "I guess it's just you and me. Daisy says she'll keep Joy here so she can sleep."

He takes my hand and tugs. "Let's go find you an SUV. Unless you'd like a minivan?"

My heart leaps at the thought of car shopping with Nick. This feels too much like something permanent. I push that thought away.

"Nope." I shake my head back and forth. "I'm not even married. I'm not buying a minivan yet."

He chuckles. "What does that mean?"

"Minivans are for soccer moms and housewives. I'm neither." I flush a little. It sounds silly, but that's how I feel.

He laughs out loud. "I never pegged you for a car snob."

I shrug my shoulders. "Whatever, Mr. Big Black Truck."

Nick throws his head back in laughter. "I guess that's fair."

We shop and shop and shop. I just can't decide. I had a certain price range in my head, but I can't seem to make the deal I'm wanting to. "Nick. I don't think I'll ever find the right car."

"You will. But you may have to compromise more than you have been. You kind of push a hard bargain, if not impossible. You're upside down on this car to be trading it in, and they know it. You'll either have to wait another six to twelve months to trade it in or bite the bullet and take the loss once you find the car that's right for you."

"I hate it when you're right." I stomp my foot. "You sound just like Dale."

"Honey." He slides his hand through my elbow. "I've been in the wheelin' dealin' business for a while. I've bought quite a few cars over the years. They're kind of my weakness."

I hate that my heart skipped a beat when he called me Honey. "This is the third car I've owned. I kind of drive them 'til they stop running. And fortunately, in the past, that's always been after they were paid off. But, if you think that's the way to go, I'll do it. I don't like driving Joy around in my little tin can, as you like to call it."

He clears his throat. "May I?"

"May you what?"

"May I talk to the next dealership?" What does he think he can do that I can't just because he's a man?

"Really?"

"Do you want to get the best deal, or not?"

Definitely, and I'm sick and tired of going back and forth. The haggling gives me a headache and a half. "Yes."

"Well, then. Follow my lead. And whatever happens, you've got to play along."

I'm getting desperate. "Alright, fine."

We pull into a much smaller car lot. "This guy may not have as many cars, but he's a good guy. He's honest. I've done my homework. I was considering changing vehicles myself, and it's important to know who you're dealing with." He hops out of the truck. He jogs around to my side, opening my door. He holds out his hand to me and helps me out. He loops his arm through mine and we walk inside. The man approaches.

"May I help you?"

"Yes. My fiancé, here, would like to buy a bigger car. We're thinking about starting a family soon, and I just don't like the idea of her riding around with our children in her tiny car. I'd like her to have something a little bigger and heavier, something more secure."

"Okay. Are you looking for a brand-new vehicle?"

"We're considering used, but not too many miles."

"Okay. And who will be signing the loan papers?"

"We both will." I go to open my mouth to speak, and Nick squeezes my hand hard. "Won't be long and we'll be married, anyway. What's yours is mine, ain't that right, darlin'?"

I nod my head stupidly, and we look back at the car salesman, who looks eager to please.

"Let's see what we have on the lot."

Nick and I follow him outside, and I see it. It's a cream-colored Honda Pilot. That's the one I want.

Nick's watching me. "How about that Honda Pilot over there? What can you tell me about it?"

We spend too much time in my opinion, talking shop about the car.

I butt in. "Can I drive it now?"

Nick laughs. "I guess we'll be test driving it."

The man hands him the keys, which I take from his hand.

"Nick. Darling. I'll be the one driving the car, so shouldn't I do the test drive?"

The car drives like a dream, and I'll pay anything to get it, which must show as I climb out of the car back at the lot. Nick looks at me, gives a little shake of his head, which I pointedly ignore as the salesman starts leanin' on me with his words. "What's it going to take to get you two into this car?"

Nick answers before I can. "I'd like to take some time to think about it. Shall we go, honey?"

I want to argue, but I'm not doing it in front of the salesman. I follow Nick outside. As soon as we're around the corner, I pull the car over to the side of the road. "Nick. I want that car."

"I know you do. But let's at least look up the Blue book value on it and compare it to the cost of the car. And you've got to call your bank to see what kind of loan you can get on it, what the interest rate is. Then you need to call your insurance guy and find out what the difference will be on an SUV with your insurance. You need to know all of this first before you even consider buying a car."

I sigh, already feeling a headache coming on. "How bout we get married, and you can make all these phone calls for me?"

"Okay, sure. At least I'll know why you're marrying me. So I can make all the important phone calls." He shoots me a grin.

I sigh. "It's a deal."

He hands me his phone. "There's the blue book value. I guess his sale price isn't that far off."

I pick up my phone and call the bank. I take down the information on a post-it note from my purse. Then I call my insurance provider and write that down too. I look through my phone notes to see what my insurance rates are now. I bite down on my pencil.

"There would be an increase, but it's one I think I can handle." I slap my forehead. "I haven't even considered the cost of Joy's daycare yet. I haven't had to. I'll need to add that to my monthly payments."

"You would, wouldn't you?" Nick looks at me in wonder. "You'd figure out a way to pay for Joy's daycare, no questions asked."

"Well, yeah. But not until I checked out the centers. I was going to do that tomorrow. Do you want to go with me?" I really hope he says yes, as this is all new territory.

"Let's hold off on that. We have time. I mean, Daisy said she'd watch her. Besides, tomorrow is the community baking event."

"Right." I can't believe I forgot. "Sorry. I guess I've just been distracted."

"Maria. If you really want that Pilot, I'll go back with you now to get it. But, if you want to sleep on it, and double check everything, I think it'll still be there tomorrow."

"I really do want it, Nick. It's the perfect car. But, if you think I should wait a few days, I will." I can't believe my words. Ordinarily I would go right back in there and buy it, but I've got Joy to think of now. I'm a mom now, which means I have to curb my impulses, starting with the man beside me.

Chapter Twenty-Five

The rest of the day, I hang out at the house with Joy. I think about Nick and what he said. Something's different, but I'm not sure what it is. Why did he tell me to hold off on finding her a daycare? Does he plan to make good on his old threat of moving away with her? He'd be within his rights to do so. But today went so well. Surely that's not what he meant. All of this worrying is giving me a stomachache. It's a relief when Daisy comes in my room, interrupting my thoughts.

"Maria! You've got to help me out! Tomorrow has got me panicked! What if I mess things up?"

"You're worried?" I can't help but laugh. "You can pull this off! You're unsinkable!"

"Thanks for your confidence." She grins at me. "It means a lot to me. But can you help me plan? That would make me feel so much better."

We spend the rest of the day planning for her cooking debut tomorrow at the center. I think we're done when she hands me a grocery list.

"You waited until now to give me this? It's a mile long!"

"I guess I've been distracted with all my shenanigans." She

shrugs. "You can do it. I have faith in you. Here's a blank check. Just bring me the receipt."

"I'd better go then." I jump up. "This is going to take me all night."

I dash to the store, feeling frantic. No sooner am I inside than I run into Richard. I must look quite the sight, as he takes pity on me, and it isn't long and we're working as a team after he snaps a picture with his phone. Having a partner cuts the shopping time in half, and he checks them off as we ring them up. He gives my cart a tap. "Good luck tomorrow, Maria."

"Thanks, Richard. I'm going to need it!"

My bags take up quite a bit of space on the kitchen floor.

"Now." Daisy stands with her hands on her hips. "The next step is to sort everything out according to the recipes. We need to separate them into boxes to make them easier to find at cooking time."

"How long will that take?" I glance at my watch. "It's ten o'clock now."

"All the better reason to hustle. Now let's get crackin'."

Blessedly, Joy manages to sleep through all our kitchen racket.

"Daisy. Now it's midnight. You going to be able to function tomorrow?"

"Maria." She clucks her tongue at me. "You worry too much. It's one night. I'm so excited for tomorrow, I wouldn't have slept much anyhow! I sure hope we have a good turnout."

"Daisy." I nod confidently. "With all the work the girls and Nick have done, I'm sure we will. Don't you worry about that."

I scoop up a sleeping Joy from the playpen and carry her back to my room. I lie her down in my bed. I change into my jammies and lay down beside her, taking out my phone.

I find myself staring at the picture in my phone that I've touched so many times. If it were a photograph, it'd be fingerprinted many times over. Nick is in his uniform, looking directly into the camera, but it's like he's looking at me. His sexy smile lights his face, and his dark brown eyes sparkle with mischief. How I miss that look. His calm, cool, reserved manner he's had around me lately is certainly more comfortable, but it's not my Nick.

Morning comes and I hear Daisy bustling up and down the hall. I feel her frantic panic seeping into my room. I hop out of bed. "Daisy. It's 7:00 a.m. What are you doing?"

"I can't sleep. I'm just so nervous. What if it's a big flop? What if the oven doesn't work right? What if the kids find me boring?"

"Don't be ridiculous. Everything will be fine. They'll all love you, just like I do. It's for a good cause. Besides, Nick and Thomas will be there. Those girls will be so distracted with those two, they won't notice any mistake you make. You've got this. Please, go back to bed. Don't get up again until eight. Try to rest."

To my relief, Joy is still sleeping, and I crawl back under the covers with her. She curls up into me, all snuggly and warm. I can't even think of what it would be like if she wasn't here. I close my eyes. I try to relax and match my breathing with hers.

An hour later, my alarm goes off. I drag myself out of bed again. I race off to shower. I smell eggs and coffee, which brings back the mornings with Nick at the stove. I sigh as I head toward the smell. I blink twice as I see him standing there. "Nick. Hey."

"Morning, sleepyhead. Ready for breakfast?"

"Oh, yeah. Thanks." I walk over and grab an empty plate and step up beside him and set it down. My arms go around his waist, and I lean into him. He feels so nice. "I'm so glad you're here."

He leans over and kisses the top of my head. "Me too."

I let go of him and get some eggs and shuffle over to the coffeepot. The eggs taste perfect. I take my plate to the sink. I pause and stare at the back of Nick. He looks so right standing in the kitchen. He belongs here. He and Joy are my home. Why did it take me so long to figure this out, and what am I going to do about it?

Nick turns around and catches me looking at him. "You'd better hurry up and get ready. Daisy's about to come unglued. We've got to get down there. Joy's staying here with Dale. He's bringing her down later. Thomas is at the hotel. I've got to leave soon and go pick him up."

"Yes. Right." I race off down the hallway.

There's a knocking on my bedroom door. "Maria. Are you decent? We need to go. Now."

"Alright, Daisy. I'm coming."

"Don't forget all my boxes."

"I won't. Just go out to the car already. I'll get them all. You should not be lifting them."

We get to the community center in record time. I can hardly believe my eyes when I walk in. The Christmas tree we decorated at the youth center is here. Nick and Thomas are here, along with about fifteen more soldiers. And they're all in uniform, including Nick. The tables are all up and decorated like Christmas, including the Christmas Jars. There's a pamphlet on each table, giving details about their significance. In the heart of it all, is Nick. He's talking to his men, giving them instructions. He catches me looking at him, and he gives me a wink.

It isn't long, and the teenagers start pouring in. I can't believe how many there are, most of them girls. There's more than a few pink cheeks heading into the kitchen to bake with the soldiers.

Abby and Eva come running over. "Maria! It was too easy!

All we did was post a few pics on our Instagram, Facebook, and our twitter accounts. Can you believe it?"

I look at Eva's phone, seeing the pictures of Thomas and Nick together. I remember being a teenage girl once. "Yes. I can."

Eva snatches her phone back.

"Maria. You can only have one of them." She sticks out her tongue, her signature face, and they run off laughing. This many kids makes me wonder if we have enough supplies. I head to the kitchen to find out.

If I had any doubts about Daisy and her presentation, I don't now. She handles these kids like a pro, barking out orders left and right. She's got them divided into stations. She lays down instructions at each station. For a minute, I forget what I'm after. "Daisy. Do you have enough groceries?"

"Thank you, yes. I've done the calculations."

"Let me know if that changes."

I leave the kitchen and leave Daisy to her fun. I walk around the room slowly, marveling at the meticulousness that went into these decorations. The room looks amazing. Nick walks over.

"Well. What do you think?"

"I think it's amazing. How did you…?"

"I had lots of help. Eva and Abby are quite the little decorators. And they brought reinforcements in the form of Roman and Rafael. Oh, and Abby's sister, Isabel, drove them back and forth and to the store, to the youth center, etc., saved me a lot of time driving, that's for sure. And then my guys did all the heavy lifting."

"I don't know what to say, Nick. It's…it's just beautiful. It's more than I could ever have envisioned." I giggle. "Who knew that paper snowflakes, Valentine hearts, flowery doilies, and blue marble stones in Mason Jars could work as Christmas decorations?"

"Where there's a will, there's a way, Maria. Isn't that what you're always telling us?" Eva pops up at my side. "Abby and I raided the spare room at the youth center. All of these decorations came from there."

"You girls certainly are resourceful." I look around the room again. "It looks fantastic."

Eva grins. "Thanks." She wanders back to Abby.

"Well, I guess I just needed inspiration." Nick gives me a smile. "We make a great team, Maria, don't you think?"

I'm overwhelmed. "I'm just so thankful, Nick. It was a suggestion, and you took it, and turned it into all this. I'm so…it's just wonderful. It's beyond wonderful. I'm truly touched." I turn away from him and wipe my eyes.

He wraps an arm around my shoulders, squeezing. "I didn't mean for you to cry."

"These are tears of joy, Nick. They're happy tears. I've never had anyone do anything like this for me or believe in me like you do."

"Maria. I…"

"Yo, Nick!" Thomas's voice carries across the room.

"You'd better answer. See what Thomas needs, he's paging you."

"Yeah. He'll be hollering again if I don't get over there pronto. I'll talk to you later. Stick around, okay?"

I smile back at him. "I wouldn't miss it for the world."

My eyes follow Nick as he makes his way through the crowd. He smiles and shakes hands as he heads to the back-storage room to help Thomas.

A familiar aroma from the kitchen drifts through the building as Daisy's baking magic fills the air. I get out the camera and start snapping pictures. I hope I get at least a few that are worthy of all their hard work.

Finally, it's bake-sale time. The bakers and their friendly smiles all man the tables filled with Christmas cookies and the Christmas Jars. The doors open, and the people pour in. If I had any doubts about a turnout, they've disappeared. Now the only thing I wonder is if they made enough cookies for everyone here. Another door opens and a bunch of kids pour in, bearing more cookies?

Dale shakes hands with a man who seems to be leading the procession of the kids and their cookies. I have a moment of panic, as all the tables are filled. The kids work quickly and efficiently. They set up a few more tables, grab an extra jar off a counter and a few brochures. Their tables are ready in minutes. Dale ambles over to me with Joy. "I thought you might need a few extra hands. I called up an old friend of mine, Matt Holden. He's all about community, and he's always willing to help. These are some of his 4-H kids. They heard there was a community event, and they dove right in."

"Thanks, Dale." My eyes tear up again. "I don't know what to say."

Dale smiles down at me. "Well, it looks like someone else has something to say." He gestures to the front of the room.

Nick stands on a small platform. He holds the microphone. He scans the crowd until his gaze stops on me. "Everyone, may I have your attention, please. My name's Nick Laus. As you may have seen on the Internet through twitter, Instagram, Facebook, and whatever other means, my two social media wizards, Eva and Abby, use, this is a community bake sale put on by the youth center under the experienced tutelage of my favorite baker, Daisy.

"The Christmas Jars on the tables are there to collect all proceeds from today's bake sale. The money collected will then be redistributed throughout the community during this holiday season for those who could use a little extra cash during these hard times. Any free-will donations in the jars are also welcome. After today, there will be a Christmas Jar at every business in town, and they will stay out until Christmas Day. It's our hope to work together as a community to reach out and help each other. Today's bake sale started as a small dream of someone here today, inspired by the movie *Christmas*

Jars. Maria Marquez had the idea, spoke it out loud, and then me and a few others just kind of ran with it. Thank you all for coming here today, giving generously, and being a part of our dream."

Nick heads back to the kitchen, and I follow.

"Nick your words were perfect. You're a great public speaker."

"I meant every word. Maria. You have to know I did this all for you. I tried to tell you something earlier."

"What's that?"

"Maria. I love you."

I hear his words, but they're too good to be true. I'm speechless. My hands fly to my face to wipe my tears.

His hands go to my hips. He grips them just a little. He clears his throat. "This isn't going to be anywhere near the impressive level of the famous Toby's NFL draft Deadpool proposal that recently went viral, but I mean every word. I love you, Maria. I want to marry you."

I press my forehead to his chest. My hands clutch his biceps. "Are you sure?"

"What do you mean, am I sure? I was in the army for twenty years. Do you think I don't know what commitment means?"

"Well, no."

Nick goes down to one knee. He winces. He's obviously in pain.

"Are you okay?"

He looks up at me. "Shrapnel and cement don't mix is all." I giggle. His serious face returns. "Maria. Will you marry me and put me out of my misery?"

I look into his eyes. I see the truth shining in them. I say the words that come from my heart, words I've kept locked up, because I was too afraid to let them out. "Yes, Nick. I'll marry you. You've brought Joy and happiness back into my life. I love you."

Epilogue

One year later…

"Nick! Come quick! I need you." My handsome husband rushes into our bedroom, where I lay nursing Hope. "Faith is hungry. Could you get her a bottle, please?" He scoops her up in his arms, cradles her against his chest, and hums her a Christmas tune. Joy toddles out of the room after her father, chattering away.

I pick up my diary from the bedside table.

Dear Diary,

It's been a while since we've visited, and this might be the last entry for at least eighteen years.

As I look into my daughter's eyes, I can't believe my life some days. Nick and I were married on Christmas day, and as Daisy said, it was only fitting that I marry my (Saint) Nick Laus on Christmas. He really is pretty great. He's always there when I need him; and I couldn't ask for a better father to our three daughters.

We weren't married long when he set out to prove my theory wrong about not carrying my own baby. Nine months later, we had two beautiful twin girls, Hope and Faith. They look a lot like their sister Joy did when she was a baby. She's such a great big sister. She hovers over them like a little mama. She loves to give them kisses.

When maternity leave is up, I suppose I'll go back to working days as a nurse, three on and four off. Daisy and Dale plan on watching the girls on those days as we still share a house with them. Nick and a few of his army buddies have slowly remodeled our home, adding on a few more bedrooms in their spare time.

I'm so proud of Nick for stepping into the job of the new director at the L. J. Youth Center. He keeps those kids hopping with all kinds of projects; the result of our brainstorming sessions we enjoy when we grab a few quiet moments and scribble down notes.

I know my entries have fallen by the wayside, but that's because I've been too busy enjoying real life to write much anymore."

-Maria

Nick is back. The bed shakes as he plops down beside me. "Morning, beautiful." He glances over at my diary. "What are you writing now?"

I look at him, all smiles. "I was writing about our life together."

"Oh? Anything interesting?"

I thump him with the book. "Weddings and babies; dreams I didn't know I had but wouldn't change for the world."

He raises his eyebrows. "Babies, huh? That's something I can help with."

I can't help but laugh. "Seriously, Nick? I haven't bathed in like three days."

He runs his finger down my calf. "You're still gorgeous to me."

I laugh as I flick his hand away. "I sure don't feel it. I haven't washed my hair in three days, which is also the last time I changed my robe."

"Let's remedy that." He lays Hope down on the bed and takes Faith out of my arms. "Go on, go hop in the bath. You get thirty minutes. I've got this. But if you come out smelling all flowery and light, all bets are off."

"Nick. I can't believe you! We have three daughters under the age of three, and you're still after my body?"

"Ah, honey. You oughtta know this soldier by now. I'll always be after your body."

I take my diary in the tub with me and settle into the flowery bubble bath.

My Dearest Liz,

I can't help but wonder if you're not smiling down on me, as I've finally figured out that life is for the living, and true love from a good man is a rare thing. My life is full, and I'm so thankful. It all started with a little Joy.

-Maria

THANK YOU FOR READING

Don't miss out on your next favorite book!

Join the Satin Romance mailing list
www.satinromance.com/mail.html

Did you enjoy this book?

We invite you to leave a review at your favorite book site, such as Goodreads, Amazon, Barnes & Noble, etc.

DID YOU KNOW THAT LEAVING A REVIEW...

- Helps other readers find books they may enjoy.
- Gives you a chance to let your voice be heard.
- Gives authors recognition for their hard work.
- Doesn't have to be long. A sentence or two about why you liked the book will do.

About the Author

I'm a thankful wife of a wonderful and loving husband, and a blessed mom of three amazing children. I'm also a grateful nurse who has the privilege to work with some pretty great people every day.

I live in the Flint Hills of Kansas. I enjoy reading and writing in my spare time. I love meandering through bookstores and libraries. I love traveling, especially to the ocean. I love meeting new people and experiencing new places. I love baking in a quiet kitchen.

I enjoy watching romantic comedies and I'm a huge fan of "The Office."

I believe a good book is a great opportunity to welcome a new perspective.

facebook.com/RachelAnneJonesAuthor

twitter.com/Jones1974Ra

instagram.com/diari1974

Also by Rachel Anne Jones

With Fire & Ice Young Adult Books

Marmalade, Uncapped